THE MOORS

BERNARD TAYLOR was born in Swindon, Wiltshire, and now lives in London. Following active service in Egypt in the Royal Air Force, he studied Fine Arts in Swindon, then at Chelsea School of Art and Birmingham University. On graduation he worked as a teacher, painter and book illustrator before going as a teacher to the United States. While there, he took up acting and writing and continued with both after his return to England. He has published ten novels under his own name, including *The Godsend* (1976), which was adapted for a major film, and *Sweetheart, Sweetheart* (1977), which Charles L. Grant has hailed as one of the finest ghost stories ever written. He has also written novels under the pseudonym Jess Foley, as well as several works of nonfiction. He has won awards for his true crime writing and also for his work as a playwright. It was during his year as resident playwright at the Queen's Theatre, Hornchurch that he wrote *The Godsend*. *There Must Be Evil*, his latest true crime study, is to be published in England in September.

MARK MORRIS has written over twenty-five novels, among which are *Toady*, *Stitch*, *The Immaculate*, *The Secret of Anatomy*, *Fiddleback*, *The Deluge* and four books in the popular *Doctor Who* range. His recently published work includes the official movie tie-in novelisation of Darren Aronofsky's *Noah*, a novella entitled *It Sustains* (Earthling Publications), which was nominated for a 2013 Shirley Jackson Award, and three new novels: *Zombie Apocalypse! Horror Hospital* (Constable & Robinson), *The Black* (PS Publishing) and *The Wolves of London*, book one of the *Obsidian Heart* trilogy (Titan Books).

BY BERNARD TAYLOR

NOVELS

The Godsend (1976)★
Sweetheart, Sweetheart (1977)★
The Reaping (1980)
The Moorstone Sickness (1982)★
The Kindness of Strangers (1985)
Madeleine (1987)
Mother's Boys (1988)
Charmed Life (1991)
Evil Intent (1994)
Since Ruby (1999)

NONFICTION

Cruelly Murdered: Constance Kent and the Killing at Road Hill House (1979)
Perfect Murder: A Century of Unsolved Homicides (1987) (with Stephen Knight)
Murder at the Priory (1988) (with Kate Clarke)
There Must Be Evil (*forthcoming*)

THE MOORSTONE SICKNESS

BERNARD TAYLOR

With a new introduction by
MARK MORRIS

VALANCOURT BOOKS

Dedication: This is for Rick Ferreira

The Moorstone Sickness by Bernard Taylor
Originally published in Great Britain by Judy Piatkus in 1982
First Valancourt Books edition 2015
Reprinted from the 1982 St. Martin's Press edition

Published by Valancourt Books, Richmond, Virginia
http://www.valancourtbooks.com

All Valancourt Books publications are printed on acid free
paper that meets all ANSI standards for archival quality paper.

ISBN 978-1-941147-83-2 (*trade paper*)
Also available as an electronic book.

Cover by M. S. Corley
Set in Dante MT 10.5/12.6

INTRODUCTION

There's just something about 1980s horror fiction.

Maybe it's because it was the decade in which I first began writing seriously, with a view to getting published, that I love it so much. Or maybe it's because it combines the traditional sensibilities of horror from an earlier period – often rural, often occult-based, often steeped in ancient lore – with a new, raw, exhilarating penchant for lurid imagery and shock tactics: the bucolic meets the brash, the ghostly meets the ghastly. It's probably partly (or mostly) my own perception, but at the time the horror I was reading in the '80s seemed to me less like a natural progression and more like a seismic shift, a leap into a brave new world.

Having said that, it would be naïve of me to claim that the only thing that exists between, say, Dennis Wheatley's stodgy black magic potboilers on the one hand and Clive Barker's startlingly graphic tales on the other is a dark, howling chasm. Even if we concentrate solely on British horror fiction, there is plenty of material to bridge the gap. We have the Pan and Fontana books of horror and ghost stories, which combined older, oft-reprinted tales from the likes of Ambrose Bierce and Algernon Blackwood with newer, more lurid offerings from young writers like David Case and Mary Danby. We have a plethora of strange, unsettling stories by Robert Aickman and a young Ramsey Campbell, which appeared in anthologies and collections throughout the '70s. And, of course, in 1974 we have James Herbert's startlingly gruesome *The Rats*, followed in fairly quick succession by his equally successful follow-ups *The Fog* and *The Survivor*.

And then, of course, we have Bernard Taylor.

A former illustrator, teacher and successful actor, Taylor wrote his first horror novel *The Godsend* in 1975. However it was his second book, *Sweetheart, Sweetheart*, which first grabbed my attention in the late '80s. Championed by Charles L. Grant (to whom, incidentally, I made my first professional story sale) in *Horror: 100 Best Books*, edited by Stephen Jones and Kim Newman (Xanadu Publications Ltd 1988), *Sweetheart, Sweetheart* is an effective, compelling supernatural novel about sexual obsession with a shockingly downbeat ending. Having enjoyed that, and being a sucker for British horror stories featuring paganism and ancient magic connected with standing stones, I then snapped up *The Moorstone Sickness* in preference to Taylor's other books on the basis of Steve Crisp's cover painting on the Grafton Books paperback edition, which depicts a gathering of lamp-bearing villagers around a huge, mist-shrouded stone, while a skull-like moon leers in the background.

As with *Sweetheart, Sweetheart*, the main protagonists of *The Moorstone Sickness* are a young couple, Hal and Rowan Graham, leaving the hustle and bustle of the big city to take up residence in an idyllic country village, a quiet place where everyone is friendly, everyone knows everyone else, and nothing bad ever happens.

Sinister, right?

Many horror stories of this period take as their premise the unearthing of the worm at the heart of the rosy red apple (Thomas Tryon's *Harvest Home* and Ira Levin's *The Stepford Wives* being a couple of examples that spring immediately to mind), and *The Moorstone Sickness* is no exception. As readers, of course, we know from the outset that the apple is rotten, but the fun lies not so much in trying to work out exactly what is going on (in *The Moorstone Sickness* the full horror of what is happening becomes obvious fairly quickly), but in watching the worm's gradual and inevitable emergence, and in wondering what, as a result, will happen to the story's protagonists, who for the most part remain blissfully unaware of the oncoming danger.

To maintain the tension it is important that readers *care* about the fate of the story's potential victims, and Taylor achieves this by making his characters engaging, believable and sympathetic. As a reader I found myself exhorting Hal and Rowan Graham to get out of Moorstone before it was too late, and it was their refusal and/or inability to do so that kept me feverishly turning the pages, right up until the . . .

Well, that would be telling, wouldn't it?

One other thing I like about Bernard Taylor's work, and which I feel I ought to highlight before allowing you to become entwined in Moorstone's dark spell, is the *way* he tells his stories. He has a clear, concise, straightforward writing style, which is both eminently readable and oddly nostalgic. There is an old-fashioned British restraint and elegance about his story telling, which puts me in mind of John Wyndham, another writer whose work I adore – in particular his novels *The Chrysalids*, *The Midwich Cuckoos* and, of course, *Day of the Triffids*. But the difference between Taylor and Wyndham is that there is a *nastiness* (in the best possible sense) to Taylor's work, which would never be found in Wyndham. If anything, this is Wyndham by way of the 1980 TV series *Hammer House of Horror* or Brian Clemens' seminal (to me, at least) mid-'70s series *Thriller*.

One other thing before I close. I haven't yet read all of Bernard Taylor's work, but he's such an entertaining and natural storyteller that I fully intend to. Last year I picked up a first edition hardback copy of his 1980 novel *The Reaping*, and when I next feel the urge to indulge myself in a bit of 1980s horror – as I often do – I'll pick it up secure in the knowledge that, if nothing else, I'll be in for a damn good time.

Because that's what Bernard Taylor does.

He delivers.

Mark Morris
December 2014

I

Hal glanced briefly at Rowan in the seat beside him to see
whether she too was aware of their nearness to the village.
She was. Ten minutes ago her eyes had been closed; secured
by her seat belt she had slept, knees bent sideways, heavy dark
hair falling unchecked across her cheek. Now she was sitting
upright, blue eyes bright and looking eagerly ahead. He could
guess at her emotions, the thoughts that were going through
her mind. Some of her own excitement had communicated
itself to him. They would soon be there. . . . They were starting new lives, the two of them. New. It was all going to be new.
And better.

'How are you doing?' he asked her, and she turned to smile
at him. 'Fine, just fine . . .'

He nodded, looked at his watch. Just coming up to two
o'clock. They had overtaken the removal van somewhere
south of Reading, ages ago. London now was far, far behind.
Far too, now, seemed Exeter, where they had stopped briefly
for coffee and a sandwich, afterwards travelling along the eastern edge of Dartmoor, and then striking west, driving deeper
into the moor's heart. In the village of Dartmeet they had
crossed over the river and turned south. And now there was
nothing to see but the moor, stretching out on either side of
them in endless stretches of green rolling hills and rambling
woodland where the trees stood poised for spring. It was hard
to believe that in England's narrow, overpopulated confines
such space, such peace and quiet, could still be found.

Behind him in the back seat the older woman was silent.

'So what do you think of it, Mrs Prescot?' he asked.

'Oh, I think it's beautiful,' her soft cockney voice came in
his ear, ' – just beautiful.'

Adjusting his view he glanced at her reflection in the driving mirror above his head. She sat gazing from the window.

Her brown hat had gone slightly askew, and her grey hair – which had also been carefully put in place at the beginning of the journey – was similarly, now, in need of attention.

'You're probably about ready to stretch your legs a bit, aren't you?' he said.

'Oh, I'm fine, Mr Graham,' she answered. 'Don't you worry about me.'

The way continued on, becoming more winding with every mile.

He had grown so accustomed to finding the road almost deserted that the figure coming suddenly into view around a bend gave him a terrifying start.

She was walking in the middle of the road. Rowan screamed and covered her face while he violently swung the wheel, hearing as he did so the hedgerow's trailing brambles lash the car's offside wing. 'Idiot!' he blurted out. 'What the bloody hell's she playing at!'

When the car was on a straight course again a few seconds later he looked into the driving mirror. The woman had gone from his sight now, hidden by the curve of the hedge. After only a moment's hesitation he braked and pulled the car over to the side.

'My God,' Rowan said, 'but that was close. That *stupid woman!*' She looked as if she were about to cry.

'Are you all right?' he asked. He was unbuckling his seat belt.

She nodded. 'It was just – such a shock. I didn't see how you were going to avoid her.' She breathed a deep sigh of relief, put one hand to her heart and gave a forced-looking smile. 'I shall be okay now.' Then, as he started to get out of the car, she asked: 'Where are you going?'

'I'd – I'd just like to make sure that she's all right . . .'

Rowan shrugged, then nodded. 'Fine – and while you're at it tell her she almost gave us heart attacks.'

Slamming the door behind him he moved back along the road in the direction from which they had come. It wasn't only the near-miss that had disturbed him – though that had been bad enough – it had been the sight of the woman herself. For one thing, there had been something about her expression, added to which she had appeared to be totally oblivious of the car's presence and any possible danger from it. Those things apart, though, there was something else. He was sure that he knew her face.

When he turned the bend in the road he found she was nowhere in sight. He came to a stop, looking about him. The air was so still; only the sound of birdsong broke the quiet. He began to feel foolish. What was he doing wandering along a country road in pursuit of some old woman? Because he had recognized her? Because there had been something disturbing about her appearance? Well, even so, it was none of his business. Forget it; go back to the car . . .

Then, just as he was about to turn he saw something lying in the road. A shoe. Her shoe, it must be. He stooped and picked it up. A plain little shoe in brown leather, looking to his untutored eye somewhat old-fashioned in pattern. He placed it on the grass at the side and moved forward again.

To his left a few yards further on he came to a gap in the hedge. Peering through he saw the woman walking away across the open ground. She had taken off her coat, he saw, and now it hung from her right hand, trailing carelessly over the grass.

For a moment he just stood there, then, stepping through the hedge, he called out to her:

'Excuse me – '

He waited, but she kept going, merely faltering in her stride and half turning her head for a second. He called again.

'Excuse me . . . Wait . . . just a minute . . .'

At his second call she came to halt, turning and facing in his direction. Then she was moving away again and continuing on, climbing the slope that cut off his view of the landscape immediately beyond. He noticed that both her feet were bare.

As she disappeared from his sight on the other side of the slope he went hurrying in pursuit of her once more. Reaching the top of the incline he saw that she had come to a stop some little distance away from him. There just beyond her bare feet he saw the gaping space of a wide pit, a chalkpit. She was standing with her back to him, looking out over the drop. She said, without turning, 'Please –' her voice was flat, ' – don't come any closer.'

He couldn't think of anything to say. Then at last, trying to sound casual, he said:

'I thought I recognized you – going past you in the car. I thought I recognized your face.'

She turned and looked at him. Her eyes were as dull and flat as her voice had been. He knew, though, that he hadn't been mistaken. 'Don't you remember?' he said.

'You? No, I don't remember you.'

'Yes, a few weeks ago. We met by the Moorstone post office. We talked for a minute or two. Don't you remember?'

This time she answered with only a little shake of her head. She looked to be in her late sixties. She seemed thinner than in his memory of her. Her hair, too, was different. Then she had worn it tight to her head. Now it hung loose and uncombed and straggling to her unbuttoned collar. She had let fall the coat, he saw; it lay between them on the grass. Moving forward a couple of steps he picked it up and held it out to her.

'Your coat,' he said, 'why don't you put it on . . . ?'

Another shake of the head. 'No. No, thank you.' She paused and added, 'I don't like it. And it's not mine, anyway.'

He let this pass. 'I didn't expect to see you out here, so far from the village,' he said.

'Oh?' She barely murmured it, at the same time giving a little shrug as if to say what did it matter anyway? Apart from her unkempt and rather wild appearance he could see misery in her face. And something else – bewilderment? 'Tell me,' he said, ' – what are you doing here?'

'Minding my own business.'

A little taken aback he hesitated, forced a smile and then said awkwardly:

'My name is Hal. Hal Graham.'

She inclined her head slightly at this. 'Hello, Hal Graham,' she said. She paused briefly, then went on; 'I didn't mean to be rude. I'm sorry.' Turning slightly away from him she gazed out over the moorland hills. 'I came here before on several occasions – to paint and sketch. I painted this chalkpit. And those trees there . . .' She pointed off to the right where a line of silver birches rose up on the skyline. 'I painted those too, in different lights, different moods . . .'

Silence again.

'Come back with me,' he said. 'My car is just down the road. Let me take you back home.'

'Oh, that would take too long. My home is a long way from here.' Her sudden little smile was all sadness.

Puzzled, he said: 'Come with me. We'll go back to the village.'

'No, not there.'

Helpless, impotent in the face of her cool, reasonable manner, he shook his head and looked at her pleadingly. '*Please* . . .'

'It isn't fair,' she said, 'to you, I mean – having this happen. It's not fair. I'm sorry.' Standing shoeless on the edge of the pit she looked like a lost, aging child.

'Come back with me,' he said. 'We can talk. We can relax.' He took a step towards her, then a step further, another and another. She looked down at his moving feet, and he came to a halt again, only a few yards away from her and very afraid.

'It won't do any good,' she said.

'Yes. I can help you. I want to help you.'

'It's too late. Go on back to your car. I'm sorry about all this.'

Slowly, slowly, he reached out his hand, at the same time taking another slow step towards her. For a second she shrank from him and his heart pounded as in his mind's eye he saw her body going over the edge. But then the next moment his hand had touched hers. Gently he held it. There were tears on her cheek. She looked at him imploringly and he could feel his tight throat growing even more constricted, feel his own tears streaming from his eyes.

'Oh, don't cry,' she said. 'You mustn't.'

'Then please – ' he fought to control himself, ' – please don't – '

Slowly she allowed him to draw her closer towards him. She was moving further and further away from the edge. Then, with her hand in his he was turning, leading her away and up the gentle incline. When they were at the top she stopped and he turned to look at her. Withdrawing her hand from his she said,

'You think I'm off my head, don't you?'

'No, I don't.'

'Yes, yes, I'm sure you must think that. I'm not, though.'

'Come on,' he said. 'Come with me. Your friends – they'll be anxious about you.'

She didn't move, and there was a look in her eyes he couldn't fathom.

'Please . . .' His voice trailed off. Moments went by and neither stirred nor spoke. All the while she seemed to be studying him. Then at last she gave a slow nod and, as if reaching a decision, said:

'All right – I'll come with you. But you've got to let me talk to you. You must listen to me.'

'Of course.' Gently he took the coat in both hands and held it out to her. 'Here – why don't you put this on?'

She looked at the coat as if she had forgotten its existence, almost as if she were seeing it for the first time. Then the next moment she had turned and was running back down the slope.

Even as he ran forward in a desperate attempt to catch her she had reached the edge of the pit. Her movements freezing in his brain like a slow-motion action replay he saw her stretch out her arms above her head, fingers pointing upwards to the sun. Then, like a swimmer taking the plunge feet first she leapt up and out and fell like a stone.

'Is she all right?' Rowan asked when Hal got back to the car. He didn't answer, just sat there with his head turned away. She repeated her question.

'What?' he said. ' – Yes. I imagine so. She'd gone – across the fields.'

When he turned to face her she stared at him. 'Hal,' she said, 'you look *dreadful*.'

He gave a little nod. His face was deathly pale and there were beads of sweat on his forehead. 'I've just been sick,' he said.

'Sick? But – you were okay when you got out – What caused it, d'you think? I mean, you've never been car-sick before . . . What do you think it could be?'

He shrugged. 'Who knows?' He waved a hand distractedly. 'Anyway – I shall be all right in a minute.'

Rowan continued to stare at him. He was sitting now with his clasped hands up to his chin. 'Was it something to do with that woman?' she asked.

'What?' His voice was almost sharp.

'Well – with almost hitting her, I mean . . .'

'No.' He shook his head firmly. 'Forget her. She's okay, I told you.' He paused. 'I shall be too. Let's forget it. It's time we got going again.'

' – Are you sure you're all right to drive?'

'Perfectly all right.' He straightened, turned on the ignition, set the car in motion and drove away.

Ten minutes later they had reached Crispin's House.

Crispin's House had been named, they'd been told, after the man who had built it back in the late eighteenth century. It stood on the northern edge of the village, occupying the site in the right angle of Crispin's Lane and North Road. An acre of land went with it – sufficient to promise a sense of seclusion while at the same time producing no feeling of isolation. And that, Rowan thought, was just about perfect.

A long, rectangular building of brick and stone, the house had two floors. It had been enlarged over the years and now showed clear evidence of the many compromises that had been deemed necessary. It would work, though, – Rowan knew it must – in spite of the occasional odd angles and the few minor inconveniences. She wouldn't have had it any other way.

They had purchased it through a local bank, which had managed the transaction on behalf of a certain Mr Childs – the then owner of the house who was absent from the village. How, Rowan wondered, could anyone own such a property and not choose to keep it for himself? Still, that was the concern of Mr Childs. She could only be glad that it had all worked out in favour of Hal and herself.

Now, entering the house, Rowan carried a suitcase up to the main bedroom. There she changed into her work clothes – old faded blue jeans and blouse. That done, she left the room and moved back along the passage to the far end, where she crossed the landing and entered the room near the top of the stairs. This would be Hal's study; a beautiful room with windows front and rear. If he couldn't work here, she thought, he couldn't work anywhere. The views were stunning. From the front one could look out south-west over the village and see the old houses and the spire of the tiny church. And there, too, beyond the other side, was the Stone, a great dark rock standing perched on the top of the highest hill. It was the Stone, she had learned, that had given the village its name.

Turning, she moved across the room and looked out through the rear window. Her view here took in the garden, bordered on either side by hedges and tall elms and there, away in the distance, the orchard with the woodlands beyond. Apart from the surrounding hills most of what she could see belonged to the house. One small acre. Crispin's acre. Now Hal's and hers.

She left the room, went down the stairs and out by the rear

door into the cool, sweet-scented air. With her back to the house she stood at the edge of the garden and looked about her. The trees were still bare, but the signs of spring were too positive to be portents of anything but the real thing. Daffodils stood straight and brilliant yellow at the borders of the lawn while over on the banks among the rambling shrubs the primroses lay in lush clumps – like clotted cream. Mauve, yellow and white crocuses sprang up between the cracks of the patio's flags and around the bole of the laburnum tree. Higher up in the branches of the tall elms the rooks flapped and cawed, their nests looking like fingerprints on the pale, hazy blue of the sky. This was the kind of place, she felt, where she belonged. It was like coming home. She would be happy here. And Hal would be happy too . . .

Hearing movement from the right she turned and saw Hal coming towards her from the kitchen doorway. 'I was wondering where you'd got to,' he said.

She smiled at him. 'I'm afraid I got side-tracked.'

'Well – I've brought in the luggage,' he said, 'and Mrs Prescot's making some tea.'

'Oh, good.'

'Did you see the note from Paul Cassen?'

'No . . . ?'

He grinned. 'You must have walked straight over it on your way in. He says that he and Sandra were here this morning and that they've left a few things – groceries – in a box in the garage.'

'Oh, isn't that kind of them!'

He nodded. 'I've just taken it inside. There're eggs, bread, butter, milk and so on. And he says if we need anything or have any problems just let them know.'

'They're such nice people,' Rowan said.

It was through Paul Cassen that she and Hal had come to the village in the first place.

Hal's swift rise in monetary fortune last year had freed them from so many ties. His fifth novel, *Spectre at the Feast*, had, in the words of the ads, been a runaway bestseller, enabling him to forget about trying to teach the three R's to a bunch of North London thugs and concentrate instead on his writing. His previous books had all done fairly well, but not to the degree where he would have risked giving up his regular teacher's salary. *Spectre* had done it, though. *Spectre* had promised to do so many things – including getting them away from the city. To return to the country had long been Rowan's all-consuming desire – and one which, she had begun to fear, would never be realized.

She had wanted to move not merely for her own sake but for Adam's too. London, she had been convinced, was not the place in which one should try to bring up a child – not when one had a choice, anyway. *Spectre*, at last, had brought them that choice . . .

The necessary money and desire, though, were not enough, they had soon discovered. Together they had spent many hours driving into different parts of Berkshire, Wiltshire and Kent – and always they had returned disappointed to their ill-designed Hampstead flat. Either they had been too late in their viewing or else they'd found that their expectations were simply not in line with the reality. Then, after several weeks, Hal had become bored with the fruitless excursions. Rowan had watched it happen, had feared that it would. And it was understandable, perhaps – after all, he had his writing to get on with, and once the novelty of house-hunting was gone it became only a time-consuming interruption. Added to that, he was not motivated as she was. He had always lived in cities, had known and sought no life but city life. He would have been content to stay where they were, she knew . . .

And then, when it was too late for Adam, they had met Paul Cassen.

On a rare expedition to the West End – rare for Rowan, anyway – they had fallen into conversation with the young doctor whilst sitting in a small café near High Holborn. The February-grey streets of London had seemed to Rowan as frantic as she had known they would be and she had suggested the stop less for the purpose of getting a cup of coffee than for fifteen minutes' respite from the overwhelming bustle.

The pleasantries that had started up between them and the tall, good-looking stranger who sat at the adjoining table had soon touched on the difficulties of life in the city, and it wasn't long before Hal had mentioned their abortive searches for something better. The man had sympathized and then gone on to describe his own treasured environment, a tiny Devonshire village which had been his home for the past seven years. It sounded nothing less than perfect.

Later, when he was gathering up his belongings in preparation to leave, Rowan, having put off asking the question, said: 'Could I ask you – if anything becomes available in Moorstone – I wonder – would you let us know about it . . . ?'

Cassen had smiled, looking from one to the other. 'It's a good bit further out than those other places where you've been looking. But of course I'll let you know – if I hear of anything. You'd better give me your address.'

When he had gone from the café Rowan had sat thinking over all that he had said about the village. 'It would be wonderful, wouldn't it,' she said, ' – if we could find a place there? It sounds just – lovely.' Then she sighed. 'But, as he said, it is a *very* long way. . . .' In the past Hal had limited their search to within a certain radius of London, and clearly Devonshire was way outside those limits. Now, though, he smiled at her across the table and said, 'well, I don't suppose it matters, does it? After all, I can take my work anywhere, can't I?'

Paul Cassen had telephoned just a week later. Hal took the call. After replacing the receiver he had turned, smiling, to Rowan. 'Have you got anything planned for tomorrow?'

'You know I haven't. Why?'

'How would you like to drive down to Devonshire – to Dartmoor – and look at a house?'

And now, in early April, that house, Crispin's House, was theirs.

'It's ours,' Rowan said. She turned and smiled into Hal's face. 'I can hardly believe it.'

'Believe it,' he said.

Studying him she said, 'How are you feeling now? Any better?'

'I'm fine now – really.'

'Good.'

After a moment she moved away, stepping from the flag-stones onto the lawn. Walking across the grass she stopped by the border, crouched and picked one of the primroses. As she bent her face to it she felt the touch of Hal's hand on her hair. She looked up. He was leaning over her.

'Disraeli's favourite,' she said, holding the flower before her.

'Yes, you can see why.'

Reaching up she put the stem of the flower into the button-hole of his breast pocket-flap. Head on one side she observed the effect. 'Very pretty.'

Turning her head again she looked around her. 'An acre is a lot of land. We shall need a gardener.'

'Yes, we shall.'

'We must ask Paul if he knows of anyone.' As she spoke she noticed something lying among the leaves of a trailing shrub. Stretching out her hand she picked up a child's ball. Obviously it had lain there for a long time; the colours had all faded and the rubber was brittle and crumbling.

A child was here once, she thought. Playing in the grass, in the sun.

She held the ball in both hands, looking over it into the past. 'If only we could have found this place sooner,' she murmured.

She was aware now of Hal kneeling at her side. Before her the flowers and the leaves were splintered by her tears. 'Ro – please don't,' she heard him say. His arms came around her, pulling her gently to his shoulder, and she laid her cheek against his collar and quietly wept. The only movement was of his hand as he gently stroked her hair.

After a while she straightened, took out a handkerchief and wiped her eyes. 'I shall be okay,' she said. Hal didn't speak, just looked at her. 'I'm sorry to be so – pathetic,' she said, ' – especially now – when we've only just arrived. But it was – this – ' she looked down at the ball and then around her at the surrounding garden, ' – and all this – everything. It was just suddenly – too much.'

His own eyes were misty, she saw. He nodded. 'I know how you feel . . .'

She sniffed; forced a smile. 'I'm all right now.'

He stood above her and helped her up. They remained in silence for a moment or two, then she said:

'This is a good place for us. I know it. And we won't let anything spoil it – get in the way . . .'

'No, we won't.'

She shivered slightly. 'That old woman – on the road back there. She gave me such a terrible fright.'

' – Don't think about her. That's all over.'

'Oh, it doesn't upset me now. At the time, though – seeing her there, right in front of us like that. If we'd hit her – God, that would have been too awful.'

'But we didn't, did we.'

'No, but – apart from any suffering she might have been caused – well, afterwards I was so much aware of how it would have – spoiled everything else.' She shook her head. 'Have you ever heard of anything so totally selfish?' She shrugged. 'I can't help it, though. I kept on thinking about it. If there *had* been an accident – *on our way here* – well, everything would have been ruined. All of it. Still, it was all right, wasn't it?'

'Yes, it was all right. Of course it was.'

She gave a little sigh, smiled and nodded with satisfaction. Then she looked at him, keenly. 'Are you sure *you're* all right? You look a little – preoccupied . . .'

'Do I? No, I'm okay.'

'That's good.' She took his arm. 'Come on, then, let's go in. Didn't you say that Mrs Prescot's making some tea?' She halted. 'Ah, so the gas and the water have been turned on. Great. What about the electricity?'

'Yes, that too.' They were moving towards the door near the kitchen. 'The phone hasn't been connected yet, though. And they said it would be done by noon.'

'Ah, well, they'll get round to it.'

Hal was frowning. 'I think I'll run down to the call box and give them a ring. Shake them up a bit.' He turned and started to move away.

'Oh, I wouldn't bother yet,' she said. 'Give them time. They'll get it done. We can call them later.'

'There won't be any time later. No, I'll go now – then I can be back for when all the stuff arrives. I shan't be long.'

Then he was stepping quickly around the corner of the house. A minute later she heard the car being driven away.

3

Hal had snatched at the excuse of the telephone – just to get out of the house.

He couldn't think how he had managed to keep up the appearance of calm in Rowan's presence. He had lied to her; pretended nothing had happened. But a woman had died. She had killed herself right before his eyes. She lay there now at the bottom of the chalkpit – and there he had been trying to go on as if getting the house in order had been his only concern. He couldn't have kept it up much longer.

There was a phone box near the corner, but he went past without giving it a second thought, turned left at the junction and drove east, heading for Paul Cassen's home.

He parked at the side of the large Queen Anne house, got out and rang the bell. To his relief the door was opened almost immediately. Cassen's wife Sandra stood there, a pretty blonde young woman whom Hal and Rowan had met on their first visit to the village.

'Is Paul around?' Hal asked once the greetings were over.

'Yes, he is. Come in.' She turned and he followed her through the hall into a large, graciously furnished sitting room. 'If you'd like to wait I'll go and fetch him,' she said and went away, closing the door behind her.

Hal had not been inside the house before. Now, left alone, he looked around him, his glance taking in the heavy velvet curtains, the fine, elegantly formed Louis XIV chairs. On polished surfaces he saw beautiful porcelain figures, all antique, while on the embossed wallpaper hung original oil paintings – landscapes, and portraits of unknown faces whose modes of dress placed them in periods of the past. The overall impression of the room was of a grace and style of bygone days.

As he stood there Cassen came in, his smile wide.

'Hal,' the doctor said, 'how nice to see you. How's the moving going?'

'Fine.' Hal paused. 'I – I wanted to see you – talk to you . . .'

Cassen studied him for a brief moment then waved him to a nearby sofa. 'Sit down . . .'

When Hal was seated Cassen took a chair facing him. 'Okay,' he said, 'tell me what's up. You're looking very worried.'

There was a little silence then Hal said:

'Half an hour ago I saw a woman die. A woman from the village. She killed herself. Right in front of me.'

'Dear God.' There was silence as Cassen stared at him. After a few seconds he added wearily, 'Tell me about it.'

Faced with the continuing expression of shock on the other's face Hal began to relate his story. When he had finished Cassen said: 'Do you know who she was?'

'No, I've no idea.' Hal went on then to give a description of her appearance, after which Cassen nodded.

'That's Emma Larkin. It couldn't be anyone else.' He groaned. 'The poor woman. Who'd have dreamed she'd do such a thing as that?' He covered his eyes with his hand and turned away. When he took his hand down a moment later Hal could see the anguish was still sharp on his face. 'Do you know why she did it?' he asked.

'Yes . . . She had cancer. It wasn't only that, though. Just lately she'd become rather – unbalanced . . . Oh, God – to think that she should take that way out of it all. . . .' He looked at Hal and shook his head. 'I'm not surprised that you should look so shaken – seeing such a thing happen.'

'I can't get it out of my mind,' Hal said quietly. 'She had an awful kind of – purpose about her. But no hysteria. That was the strange thing. Just this kind of – sad calm. And bewilderment too, as if she was in some kind of shock or something.' He fumbled in his pockets and Cassen got up and pushed a cigarette box across the coffee table towards him. Hal took a cigarette, lit it and exhaled the smoke. 'I'd met her before,' he said, 'in the village. The very first time we came here. It was by the post office, I remember. I was waiting for Rowan and the old lady and I just – fell into conversation. She seemed perfectly composed then. There seemed to be nothing about her then that you'd describe as – despairing in any way.' He paused. 'When I saw her today, though, she didn't remember me at all. – She told me how she used to go up there – by the pit – and paint and sketch.'

'She said that?' Cassen looked doubtful. 'No, she never painted – not as far as I know. That was just her mind wandering, I'm afraid. Her tenant was a painter. Not Emma Larkin, though.' He sighed. 'Did anyone else see her – see it happen?'

'There was only me.'

'So if you hadn't been there we wouldn't know what had happened to her. She'd be just lying out there – until somebody found her. Mind you, I'm sorry it had to be you who saw it. It's not a nice welcome for you. Anyway, thank you for telling me.' He got up from his chair. 'Now, I suppose I'd better do something about it.'

'I almost didn't tell you,' Hal said abruptly. 'I didn't want to tell anyone.'

Cassen stopped and looked at him. ' – Why not?'

Hal shrugged. After a moment he said: 'I didn't want to be – brought into it. But now I shall be, shan't I?'

'Well – you were there. You saw it happen . . .'

'Yes. And so now I shall have to go to the inquest. There's bound to be an inquest, isn't there?'

'Of course. It'll be held in the village school.' Cassen paused. 'Hal – I don't understand what this is about – what your problem is – '

Hal got to his feet and took a few paces across the room. 'The thing is,' he said, 'neither Rowan nor my housekeeper knows about it. I didn't tell them. Rowan – well, I didn't want her to know. I still don't – if I can help it.'

'About Emma Larkin?'

'Yes. Oh, I realize that in time she's bound to learn that it happened, but – oh, I can't stand the thought of her knowing that I was there – that I saw it happen – that it happened just a few yards from where she was sitting.'

'Why is that?'

Hal took a long drag on his cigarette and stubbed it out. 'She – hasn't been well . . .'

Cassen looked thoughtful. 'Sit down again,' he said, 'and tell me the rest.'

When they were facing one another from their seats again Hal cleared his throat and began, haltingly:

'We – we had a son. Adam. He was just over two years old. And then – last summer – he died.' He lowered his gaze from Cassen's face, paused, steadying his breathing. 'Near where we lived there's no really safe place for small children to play. Oh, we had a tiny piece of communal garden but vandals had wrecked the fence the week before and Rowan – well, both of us – we were afraid to let Adam play outside until it was repaired – in case he wandered into the road. For a little time past we'd been driving out into the country looking for somewhere else to live. Rowan was so against bringing him up in London. She never did care for it there – and always said it wasn't the place for a child. We hadn't found anything, though – nothing that both of us were happy with. My fault, I suppose. Apart from being just too damned hard to please I'd also lost interest in the whole idea. It just got to be too much trouble. You see, I was fairly content where we were and – ' He broke off, shook his head and sat in silence.

'What happened?' Cassen said.

'That – that particular day was stiflingly warm. There was a glazier in. We were having new windows fitted in the balcony doors. He'd been out there a couple of hours with his step-ladder and things. Adam was playing in the sitting room. Rowan was busy nearby – and keeping an eye on him. Everything was fine. And then, all of a sudden, it all went wrong. Rowan had a minor crisis at the stove . . . And it – it happened then.' His sentences were coming out even more jerkily, sometimes the words tumbling over each other and at other times disjointed. 'It – it happened all at once,' he said. 'In those couple of minutes while Rowan was occupied in the kitchen the workman went outside to his van to get some tool or other. And Adam – finding the doors to the balcony open, went out there . . . He – he got up, somehow – onto the step-ladder. Rowan – she didn't hear anything at all. There was no sound, she said. She just turned around and he wasn't there anymore. Then, in the same moment that she realized he'd gone she heard the cries of a neighbour down below.' There was silence for a few seconds, then he added dully, 'He died the same day.'

The silence fell again, broken by Cassen who at last murmured: 'I don't know what to say. In my job I see death more often than most people do, I suppose. But I *still* never know what to say. I doubt that I ever shall.' He paused. 'And this was last August . . . ?'

'Yes.'

'And since then Rowan hasn't been well . . . ?'

'No.'

'How old is she?'

'Twenty-seven.' Hal sat staring down, as if concentrating on his square-cut hands, now placed fingers spread on his thighs. The memory was much too fresh. He could still hear Ro's screams ringing out as he'd sat working in his study. 'You never saw such a change in anybody,' he said. 'Before that happened she was fine – apart from wanting to move, I mean. I was making good money. And she was working at her own writing in her spare time. It was good. We had nearly everything we wanted. And then – then *that* happened. When Adam died she just – fell apart . . .' He came to a stop.

'Go on,' Cassen gently prompted.

'She withdrew into herself.'

'In what way?'

'It was a gradual thing. At first she just didn't want to see people – to have anyone come round – or go out to see them. So – we'd just stay on our own. The only person we saw with any frequency was Mrs Prescot – she's our housekeeper now. In the end Rowan was going out less and less even on ordinary, everyday errands, shopping and so forth. Mrs Prescot was doing it all. Rowan – I don't know – she seemed afraid of going out – afraid of the people – and the city itself. I used to have the devil's own job to get her beyond the front door.'

'Did she have any medical help?'

'Oh, yes – of a sort. But what could anyone do – except prescribe pills? Nothing could get to the cause of it. *That* was beyond changing.' He shook his head. 'Oh, they were well-meaning and concerned enough – the doctors – but they couldn't really help her.'

'And how is she now?'

'She's been so much better lately.'

'She seemed to me to be all right – when I met you both that first time in the café . . .'

'Yes, well . . . a stranger wouldn't necessarily be aware. Besides, by that time we'd started again to look for another place to live. I think that made a difference to her – to have the belief that we would be getting away. One thing was certain – we couldn't stay in the flat after that – not for any length of time.' He shook his head sadly. 'If only I'd made a real effort before.'

Cassen said evenly: 'You mustn't blame yourself.' After looking at Hal keenly for a moment he added: 'And what about you? – your own state during this time?'

'What?'

'How did you manage through it all?'

'Well, I had my writing, and I just – just dived into it, I suppose. Anything not to think about him – Adam. When I look back I seem to have spent my time working all the hours God made. And of course Ro came off the loser there too.' He frowned. 'I should have been with her more. Though I don't think it was selfishness on my part. I don't think so. It was just my own – inability to cope – with any of it.'

'I understand . . .'

'And of course it affected our whole marriage.'

'I should be surprised if it didn't. And how is it now with you? With both of you?'

Hal hesitated for a second, then said non-committally: 'It's better.' Then he added: 'And it will be better still. Much better – now that we're away from London – without all the constant reminders. And if we can make a good start . . . Here – well, we both think we've found the right place to do that.'

'I'm sure you have,' Cassen smiled. 'And I'll tell you something – you won't want for support.' The smile grew warmer. 'Hal, you're both going to be very happy in Moorstone, I'm certain.'

'That's what I'm hoping. And this is a good place in which to raise a family . . .'

Silence fell between them, heightened by the ticking of the antique French clock above the fireplace. Hal said, his expression grave once more:

'But now this has happened. Just on the very day of our arrival. That poor woman . . .'

'And Rowan has no idea at all about it?'

'No.'

'Does she know where you are now?'

'I told her I was coming out to see about the phone – to get it connected. I couldn't bring myself to tell her what had happened. She was shaken enough when we almost ran the old lady down. She couldn't have coped with being told the rest of the story, I know. Not after what she's been through. It would ruin everything, I know it would. All the progress she's made. She's a different person now. I can't have her go back to how she was. And I'm afraid now – that it will happen.' He shook his head despondently. 'As I said, for a time there I thought I wouldn't tell anyone. After all, no one knew that I'd seen it; I could just forget it all; pretend I wasn't there.' He sighed. 'But in the end I couldn't. I couldn't just put it aside – as if it had never happened. I couldn't just leave that old woman out there. So – ' he shrugged, ' – I came to see you. Now, at least, I won't have that on my conscience.'

Cassen said nothing, just looked at Hal across the India-carpeted space between. After some moments of silence Hal said resignedly:

'But now that I've reported it – acknowledged it – it will all come out – my part in it all. Rowan will know everything.'

Cassen got up from his chair and went towards him. He stood looking down at him for a second, then said:

'Just leave it with me, Hal. And don't worry. Rowan's not going to be upset by this.'

'But when the – '

'I mean it. Believe me. I'll take it from here and report it to the right people. You just go on back to your house and get on with whatever work you have to do. And just remember – you know nothing about all this. Nothing at all. So just – get it out of your mind. Don't even think about it.'

Hal stood up. 'But the inquest and – '

'Don't think about it,' Cassen interrupted. He spread his hands. 'Emma Larkin is dead – and it's a terrible, terrible thing. But she *is dead*. Now, as a doctor and a humanist my immediate concern can no longer be with her. We must live for the living. As sad as it is there's nothing at all that anyone can do now to help Emma Larkin. But we can do something to help your wife. And I think it's important that we try. We don't want her having a nervous breakdown or running away as soon as she's got here.' He reached out and clasped Hal's shoulder. 'Go on home. She'll be waiting for you to give her a hand.'

Hal remained still for a moment then turned and followed Cassen into the hall. At the front door Cassen said, 'And cheer up. Believe me when I say that everything's going to be all right. Take my word for it; nothing's going to spoil Rowan's arrival here.'

There was something in the man's manner and tone of voice that Hal found calming and reassuring. He was at a loss as to what to say. In the end he just murmured his inadequate thanks and stepped through the doorway. Turning, he added: 'Oh – your note and the box of groceries you and Sandra left at the house. I haven't even thanked you for that. You must think I'm an ungrateful so-and-so.'

Cassen smiled. 'How could you thank me? You haven't seen me this afternoon.'

Hal smiled then for the first time since arriving there. 'True,' he said.

He turned again and walked towards his car. When he reached it he saw that Cassen was still standing in the porch. For a moment they looked gravely at one another, then Cassen gave an encouraging smile and called out: 'Oh, by the way, it's nice to be able to say it in person, so let me say it now: Welcome to Moorstone. Welcome home.'

4

Will Halligan, a carpenter from the village, had spent all yesterday, Wednesday, putting up shelves in Hal's study. Now, with the room swept and clean again Hal was at work unpacking and setting in order his papers, files and hundreds of books. At present the room, like most of the rest of the house, was in disorder – but then, it was only the third day; it would be all right soon – give it a little more time.

Swinging his chair back to face the large, thickly cluttered desk, he looked across it through the window onto the sunlit rooftops of the village.

'How's it going?'

Rowan's voice sounded behind him and he turned and saw her standing just inside the doorway, in her hands a tray on which stood cups and saucers.

'Fine.' He smiled at her.

'I've brought you some coffee,' she said as she came towards him. When he'd pushed aside several books to make room she put the tray down and perched beside it on the edge of the desk. While he picked up his cup she looked out at the view. 'Sometimes,' she said, 'I get so involved with all the unpacking and the sorting out that I forget where I am. Then I look around me and realize.'

'I know what you mean.' He looked up at her over the rim of his cup. Her dark hair was tied back from her face with a pale blue ribbon at the nape of her neck. Over her blouse and blue jeans she wore an apron bearing a reproduction of an old mustard advertisement. She smiled. He was well aware of the amount of work that awaited her throughout the house, but in spite of it she was looking happier and more relaxed than he'd seen her in a long while.

'As soon as I've got all this in some sort of shape I can come and give you a hand,' he said. 'You're coping okay for now, though, are you?'

'Yes, with a lot of help from Mrs Prescot.'

'Thank God for Mrs Prescot.'

'Amen.'

There was a little silence then she said, with the slightest note of self-consciousness: 'I think maybe tomorrow I'll take a walk around the village. It's time I got a better idea of what the local shops have to offer.'

'I'll come with you if you like.'

'No, you stay here and work.'

'Tote that barge, lift that bale. Thanks a lot.'

She took up her own cup, drank from it and then said quietly, 'It's different here in this place, Hal. It's not like – there.' Then she shrugged. 'But maybe it's not that. Maybe the difference is in me.'

'I would think that might be true.'

'Yes, but then again, maybe it's the village that brings it out – that difference, that change . . .'

He laid his hand on the soft roundness of her thigh. 'Don't underestimate yourself, Ro.'

'No, I won't. But the whole thing is so – oh, I don't know.

It just – feels so good here. So right.' She paused. 'And how do
you feel about it? – now that you're here?'

'Exhausted.'

'No, be serious.'

'It's a beautiful place.'

'But how do you *feel* about it?'

'I feel good.'

A moment of silence, then she said: 'But you wouldn't have
come here had it not been for me, would you?'

He looked at her. He didn't know what to answer.

What she said was true. 'Well,' he murmured, 'that's a difficult question . . .'

'Is it?' She was smiling at him, her eyes soft and slightly anxious. 'But you won't regret it, Hal. You wait till you get used to
it. When we get settled in. You'll really be glad.'

'I'm glad now.'

'Good.' She put down her cup and turned to look from the
window again. 'I'd almost forgotten what it could be like. The
peace and the – gentleness. Just waking up in the morning –
even that; waking up to the sound of birds singing instead of
cars changing gear. It's all so different.'

'I'll say. No litter all over the place. No piggish London taxi
drivers. And you can walk without stepping in dog crap every
few yards. I'm all for that.'

'And the lovely old houses. And all the space. And the people
too. They seem genuinely to care for each other. God, when I
think back – I mean, just take the milkman for example; that
surly, long-suffering old devil in London did it all as if it cost
him blood every time. Here, this one's so warm and friendly.'

'*How* warm and friendly?' Hal raised an eyebrow.

'No, really. And he's typical. He was so nice, so pleasant,
and . . . welcoming. This morning he was telling me all about
the village, and the different people. And you could tell – you
could sense the regard they have for each other. He told me
they're having a memorial service at the church on Saturday,
for one of the villagers. Everybody'll be there, he said. Yet she
wasn't famous at all or anything like that. She was just – one

of them. Loved, he said. She was loved. Can you think of any nicer tribute?'

At random Hal picked up a book and began to leaf through it. Attempting to sound casual he asked, 'Who was she?'

'I think he called her Emma Larkin or Parkin – something like that. She just died peacefully in her sleep, he said.'

After a moment he was aware of her picking up the empty cups and putting them back on the tray. 'Well,' she said, 'I'd better get back to work.'

Left alone again he sat at his desk unmindful of the chaos around him. *She just died peacefully in her sleep. . . .* So the death of Miss Larkin had been put down to natural causes. And nothing could be further from the truth. Still, such a downright lie couldn't cause her any more suffering than she had already known – and that, he reflected, must have been literally unbearable.

When he thought of the dreadful calamity – and he had done so many times – he always saw the misery and the bewilderment in the woman's face. He heard her voice again: *It isn't fair to you . . . having this happen . . . it's not fair . . . I'm sorry . . .* He thought too of the last words she had spoken: *I'll come with you . . . But you've got to let me talk to you . . . You must listen to me . . .* Most of all, though, he relived the moment – and it had taken only that – when she had run from him and leapt up and out over the edge.

Her body hitting the bottom of the pit had sounded so loud. How could such a small body make so much noise? But it was the echo, most of it was the echo, caused by the hollowness of the pit. Even so there had been a terrifying finality about the sound that for a second had held him, eyes screwed up, rooted to the spot on which he had halted.

When he had looked over the edge he had seen her body down below, looking like a discarded bundle of old clothes, dark against the chalk. Minutes later when he had found a way down to the bottom and stood immediately above her he had seen that her skirt had ridden up above her head, covering her face and exposing her thin legs. In an attempt to give her back a little of her dignity he had reached out, taken the hem of the brown skirt and pulled it down over her thighs. Her head was uncovered then. Her eyes, flat and lifeless, the lids half-lowered, had looked dully past his shoulder at the open sky. Her mouth was fixed in a silent, never-ending cry of despair. Her skull had cracked open like an egg and her blood and her brains had been mingled around her head like a halo . . .

And now that awful, grotesque ending had been passed off under a label of the most perfect serenity. *She just died peacefully in her sleep.* And, as far as Rowan was aware, *that* was the truth.

His own knowledge, though, left him with a new, small feeling of discomfort. Not at the horror of the woman's death – though that was bad enough – but at the seeming ease with which that horror had been smoothed out. But there, after all, he had got his wish. Ro had been shielded from the reality – a reality he had feared would be too much for her. He had wanted it and he had got it.

And he was grateful to Paul Cassen, of course he was. And he would always be so. It was thanks to Paul that their arrival – as far as Ro was concerned – had been unmarred by the dreadful happening. But even so . . .

Then he thought again of Paul Cassen's words to him: *Miss Larkin is dead. We must live for the living.* And surely, in the general scheme, that was what really counted. The living. That was Ro and himself. And that's what they were here for – to live – to remake their lives.

With an effort he thrust from his mind the stark pictures of Miss Larkin's broken body. She was dead. It was over. Her life had ended, but theirs – his and Ro's – were just beginning again.

He got up, walked to the rear window and looked out onto the sunlit garden. Starlings pecked and squabbled on the lawn. A robin, breast flaming, flew down and perched for an instant on the garden seat, then took off again to alight on a branch of the laburnum tree above. 'Welcome to Moorstone,' Cassen had said. 'Welcome home.'

And that's where they were. They did things differently here. This wasn't London. This was Moorstone. This, now, was home.

5

As Rowan stood at the kitchen table adding notes to the scrap of paper that was her shopping list Hal busied himself at the stove. Pausing in the act of measuring coffee into the paper filter, he asked over his shoulder whether she wanted a cup.

'No, thanks,' she said. 'I haven't got time.' She glanced past him to the window, beyond which the sky was looking increasingly grey and heavy. 'It's going to rain. I shall have to take an umbrella. Damned nuisance.' Had this been London she would have used the threatening clouds as an excuse not to venture out. Not here, though. And not anymore. From now on she was determined to keep the past where it belonged.

They had been in the house over three weeks now, and with each day London seemed further and further away. She didn't miss it in the least. Not that there had been much time anyway for thinking about places and events beyond Crispin's House and the village; here life was full. At first it had seemed that the state of chaos and flux in the house would never come to an end. Now, though, most of the disorder had gone. Places had been found for most of the items that had hung around in the boxes and the tea-chests, and what hadn't found a place had been consigned to the cellar. And the furniture was all settled as well, amongst it the pieces they had acquired along with the house, pieces which included a beautiful old grand piano and an equally beautiful old cabinet wind-up HMV gramophone. The former had had immediate attraction for Rowan – 'I shall learn to play properly now,' she had said – and the other for Hal – as a complement for his large collection of old seventy-eights. Everything, now, seemed to Rowan to be gaining a stronger look of permanence and belonging – qualities that also applied to herself, she felt, more strongly, more surely every day. With the major demands of the moving in behind them her life was gradually falling into an easy, welcome routine, like the comfort of old jeans and slippers after returning home from a formal dinner. She was at home again. She had even rediscovered her own, old enthusiasm for writing and during the odd hours over the past week had managed to jot down ideas for two or three children's stories. This Hal had further encouraged when, yesterday, he had fixed up the small room next to Mrs Prescot's as a study for her.

She watched Hal now as he in turn idly watched the coffee filtering into the pot. *She* had settled in, but how, she wondered, was *he* taking to his new environment? And it really *was* new for him. Certainly he appeared to be doing all right – and he was making every effort. Apart from all the general work he had done around the house he had also, she'd been glad to see, devoted some time to more personal concerns – having shelves built for his record collection and carefully choosing the perfect sites for the hanging of his much treasured pictures – a Wyeth painting, a Hockney drawing and a Picasso etching. Living here must be less easy for him, though, she knew. Unlike her he had never before lived in the country. Still, in her own growing contentment the present sight of him in his familiar worn jeans and darned-at-the-elbows cardigan against the uneven white-painted walls of the old kitchen already seemed more real than recalled images from their London life.

She continued, unobserved, to study him. They had met just over five years ago during a visit he had made to the small Yorkshire village in which she had lived for most of her life. He had gone there to get local colour and information for the book he'd been working on, making the library his first stop. She'd been the librarian. She could remember so well the sight of him that day – a tall, good-looking young man who had smiled at her across her little polished desk, politely asking a string of questions from a list he had held in his hand. Throughout the rest of the time he had spent there she had helped him whenever she could. She'd been glad to. She was impressed.

He hadn't headed back to London afterwards as he'd originally said he would, but instead had booked a room for himself at a small local hotel – and then returned to the library and asked her out for dinner. Later, over the meal, he had spoken of his writing – he was clearly obsessed with it – and she in turn had told him of the few children's stories she'd had published. Afterwards he had driven her back to the small cottage where she had lived alone since the death of her parents, leaving her at the door with a squeeze of the hand, a brief peck on the cheek and the expressed hope of seeing her the next day.

The following afternoon, late, after spending more time with her, he had left to return to London. But then he had written, following up his letter with a further visit. This time, though, he had stayed at the cottage, sleeping with her in her huge old bed. She hadn't cared what the neighbours, watching him arrive and leave, might think. She already knew that she loved him. Four months later they had married and she had sold the cottage and moved into his London flat.

Now as he turned to pick up his cup and saucer their eyes met. She smiled at him and he grinned back at her, brown eyes very bright, one hand lifting to brush fingers through his thick, dark, unruly hair. 'How've you been getting on?' she asked. Today had seen the first hours he'd spent back at his desk for several weeks.

'It's a bitch,' he answered, 'trying to pick up the threads again after so long – after all the disruption. And it'll take me a little time before I can really get going on it again. Still . . .'

Briefly Rowan reflected, as she had done on several occasions, that it wouldn't matter much, financially, if he didn't write anything at all for the next year or two – not after the success of *Spectre*. But he had never been one just to sit back; ever since she had known him he had been totally committed to his writing. It was a major, essential part of his life, and she could never imagine him being without it. It was, too, she had sometimes felt observing him rapt in the demands of his obsession, a part of his life that at times excluded her. Oh, yes, he shared his work with her as well as he was able – reading sections aloud, asking her opinions – but the very passion of his dedication sometimes erected a wall which no amount of verbal sharing could dismantle. Still, by now it was something she had learned to live with and accept; it was a part of him. . . .

She watched as he poured his coffee, added milk, took up the cup and moved to the door. As he opened it he said, 'Are you taking the car?'

'I think we'll have to. There's all the weekend shopping to get.' In London she had hardly driven at all. Now, though, since the move, she was getting back into practice; the streets of Moorstone held no fears for her.

'Is Mrs Prescot going with you?'

'Oh, yes.'

He paused. 'I shall miss her when she returns to London.'

'Yes, I'm sure you will. So shall I.'

Mrs Prescot had been a part of Hal's life long before she, Rowan, had entered it. For some years, in London, the older woman had gone to his flat regularly three times a week, come rain or come shine, to do his cleaning, his laundry and the odd bits of shopping and cooking. Nor had his marriage done anything to disturb the pattern, for up to the advent of Adam Rowan had had her own job during the day, in one of the city's libraries, and had also tried to continue with her own writing in any spare time. Furthermore, she and Mrs Prescot, for all their different backgrounds, had got on wonderfully well together. And so the long established arrangements had continued. Until the planned move to Moorstone, that is. That, it seemed, would see an end to it all. But then they had persuaded her to leave with them for the village and stay with them for the first month whilst they got settled into their new home. Now, following discussions, Mrs Prescot had agreed to stay on further, till the end of May.

'I can't imagine what it'll be like without her,' Hal said. 'Still, now that she's given us a reprieve we'll have time to get things sorted out and find somebody else. It shouldn't be too difficult. I had a word with Paul Cassen about it – just a couple of days ago – and he mentioned somebody who he thought might be suitable.'

'Oh?'

'Some woman from the village. Apparently she's looking for a post as a housekeeper. He recommended her very highly. I've forgotten her name now.'

Rowan shrugged. 'It doesn't matter, anyway – since Mrs Prescot's staying on for a while. Still, we can keep the other woman in mind for later on – that is if we decide then that we still need someone. I'm not sure that we shall.'

When Hal had left to return to his study Rowan glanced back to the window. The sky was looking even darker. She got her raincoat. As she stood buttoning it Mrs Prescot appeared. All ready to leave, she too was dressed for rain.

As they emerged from the house and made for the garage the rain began to fall. Mrs Prescot put up her umbrella and then said with a little click of her tongue: 'If it's raining in London I hope my sister's not out in it.' She turned to Rowan with a wry smile. 'I came away with Kath's umbrella.'

With their full shopping bags loaded into the boot of the Renault the two women made their way back along the narrow pavement towards the High Street once more. There was little more for them to do now and with luck they would be finished before the rain came down again. After its half-hearted beginning it had held off. Now, though, the sky was looking increasingly threatening with every minute.

The only thing still remaining for Rowan was to change her books at the library. 'That won't take me long,' she said as they reached the corner. 'What about you?'

'Just the chemist's and the post office.'

'Fine, well when you've finished, meet me in The Coffee Shop.' Rowan indicated a small café some little way down the street. 'We'll relax for ten minutes before we go home.'

Mrs Prescot nodded and started away while Rowan moved off in the opposite direction.

The library was a solid grey stone building on the far side of the green. It was, Rowan had discovered on a previous visit, surprisingly well stocked for such a small village. Also, she had found to her pleasure that the catalogue listed all of Hal's novels, including two copies of *Spectre*. Added to that, all his books were out on loan. Clearly, since arriving in the village he had become something of a celebrity.

After handing in the books she had read, she wasted no time in making a further selection and taking them to the counter. There was a young woman standing in front of her, waiting with ill-concealed impatience for her own books to be stamped and replying with curt monosyllables to the pleasantries of the librarian, a tall, good-looking, red-haired man who was taking his time. As Rowan watched, the girl held out her hand, palm flat, waiting for him to finish with her books and return them to her. 'I don't know whether you've noticed,' the girl said, 'but you've got another customer waiting.' Unsmiling, she took the books he then held out to her, put them into her bag, turned, and without another word, went away.

When Rowan's books had been stamped she thanked the man and headed for the exit. As the door swung shut behind her she saw the young woman standing within the shelter of the porch. The rain was coming down again, with such force that it was bouncing up off the paving stones.

Rowan began to raise her umbrella then closed it again and lowered it to her side. With a shake of her head she said:

'Sometimes an umbrella's just not enough, is it? I mean, it's fine for your head, but what do you do about your feet?'

The girl turned to her. 'You're lucky you even thought far enough ahead to bring an umbrella. I'm afraid I just dashed out – and now I'm paying the penalty.' She was close to Rowan's own age, Rowan thought. Maybe a little younger; maybe twenty-four or twenty-five. She wore a tan trenchcoat. Her straight fair hair was worn in a long pageboy trim. Her eyes were blue. She was, Rowan thought, extremely pretty.

'I think,' said the girl after a moment, 'that you must be Mrs Graham – Rowan Graham, right?'

'Why, yes, I am, but –'

'Oh, there's no mystery as to how I know.' The girl's smile was warm and open. 'It's common knowledge here that the

Grahams have recently moved in – and what they look like. So, as you fit the description and I've never met you before – well, I put two and two together.' She paused, then added: 'My name is Alison. Alison Lucas. Like you, I'm a newcomer to Moorstone.'

'Oh, really? How long have you been here?'

'A little over five weeks.'

'Only a fortnight longer than we have.'

The girl waved a hand, indicating the south-western part of the village. 'I'm staying on Moorstone Road – working for Edith Carroll.'

'I'm sorry – ' Rowan shook her head, ' – I don't know her. But we haven't met that many people and – '

'Oh, I just thought you might have recognized the name – your husband being a writer. She's a writer too.'

'Oh, yes, of course.' Rowan nodded. 'Doesn't she write historical novels and that sort of thing?'

'That's right. And big, sprawling family sagas. All with period settings. I suppose you'd call me her secretary. I do her typing for her – when there's anything to type – and her filing and so on. Though, really, just as much, I'm here as a sort of companion. She doesn't get through much in the way of actual writing. Well, she's getting on – probably slowing down a bit.'

'Do you enjoy the work?'

'Oh, I can't complain about it at all. It's a very easy life. She makes it all very comfortable for me. Lots of free time when I want it. My only task for the whole morning has been to collect some books from here.' She grinned wryly. 'And wouldn't you know I'd have to choose a time like this.'

The rain was falling even harder now. Everyone seemed to have been driven off the streets. Looking out at the pelting drops and the deepening and widening puddles, Rowan said: 'It looks as if you're going to be marooned here. Wouldn't you be more comfortable waiting inside until it eases?'

The girl shook her head. 'No, thanks. I'd rather be uncomfortable than risk another meeting with Mr Collins.'

'Who?'

'Ralph Collins – the librarian. The character at the desk.'

'Oh, dear. Is he giving you problems?'

'He would if I let him. No, he's just a pain in the neck. The trouble is he seems to have taken a shine to me – and he just won't take no for an answer. The fact that I've told him, A, I'm married, and B, that I'm not at all interested in him, doesn't seem to touch him in the slightest. I hate coming here to the library – simply because of him. Mind you, he visits Miss Carroll's quite frequently, so I do have difficulty in avoiding him.' She shook her head. 'Ah, well, he'll take the hint sometime, I suppose. I *hope*.'

Looking out onto the street again Rowan saw that the force of the rain was lessening. 'I'm supposed to be meeting my housekeeper at The Coffee Shop,' she said. Then she added: 'Listen, if you're not in that much of a hurry why don't you come and have a coffee with us? We could dash round now – while it's not too heavy . . .'

'Well, I'd love to – if you're sure I wouldn't be in the way.'

'No, of course not.' Rowan smiled and glanced briefly up at the sky. 'I think it's now or never,' she said. 'Are you game?'

'I'm game.'

Rowan raised her umbrella over them both. They turned to one another for a second, smiling like old friends, and then dashed out onto the pavement and hurried away, heels ringing on the wet slabs. Two minutes later they had reached the door to the café.

As Rowan followed Alison inside she almost collided with a tall, dark man who was emerging onto the pavement. He apologized to her and went on his way, and for a moment she stood gazing after him. Then, turning again, she placed her umbrella in the stand near the door and looked around her. There was no sign yet of Mrs Prescot.

Although the café was busy the two girls were lucky enough to find a window table that had just that second been vacated. They moved over to it, hung up their coats and sat down. Alison took out her cigarettes and offered them to Rowan. 'No, thanks.' Rowan shook her head. 'I don't smoke.'

Alison took a cigarette for herself and lit it. Rowan said: 'Did you notice that man I nearly bumped into as we came in?'

'Yes.' Alison was smiling at her. 'And I know what you're going to say.'

'You do?'

'Yes. You're going to say that he looks like the actor David Lockyer . . .'

'You're right.'

Alison nodded. 'He was.'

'Was?'

'It *is* David Lockyer, and I mean he *was* the actor. Not now, though. He's given all that up. Now he concentrates on music. He's a composer. Been here a couple of years now, so I'm told. He writes music for films and television – that sort of thing. And very successfully, too, by all accounts.'

'But – but what about his acting career? Has he given all that up?'

'So it would seem.'

Rowan nodded slowly. 'So that's why he hasn't done anything in that line for a while. But he was so popular, what with the television series and the various West End plays. I remember reading an interview with him when he talked of how he'd had to work to get where he was – and how satisfying the whole thing was.' She shook her head in wonderment. 'And now he's just – given it all up.'

'People are weird, aren't they?' Alison was looking around for the waitress. 'Apparently he doesn't even talk about it now – his past; he won't. Just not interested in it anymore.'

'He used to live in London, I remember reading. But now you say he lives here . . .'

'Yes, he's got a house in the High Street – just across the road from The Swan.'

Rowan grinned. 'You know a lot about what goes on in Moorstone.'

Alison smiled back and shrugged. '*Everybody* knows what goes on in Moorstone. It's hard to keep secrets here.'

The waitress came over then and they ordered coffee.

When she had gone Rowan asked: 'Did you come to the village on your own? – You mentioned that you're married . . .'

'Yes, I did come here on my own. My husband, Geoff, is working abroad. Saudi Arabia. He's helping build a palace or something for one of those rich Arab princes. He's going to be away for a year.'

'Ah, well, that's not too long.'

'Isn't it?' Alison smiled. 'It seems a hell of a long time to me.'

'Where were you before you came here?'

'Our home's in Brighton. I was getting a bit restless there – on my own and between jobs. So – I decided to get away. And I did. I let the house to some eager visiting Americans and came here.'

'Didn't you want to go out there with him – your husband?'

'Oh, I could have done but it seemed hardly worth it. As he's not there for very long – and not living too comfortably at that – so he says. If he were staying longer – well . . .' She smiled. 'God, but I miss him. That's one of the reasons I took this job – because I was missing him so much; I thought a change of scene would be a nice diversion.'

'How long have you been married?'

'Three years.'

'And you'll be staying here till Geoff has finished his contract out there?'

'Oh, yes. I've told Miss Carroll I shall.' She shrugged. 'I suppose the time will pass – eventually.'

After the waitress had brought their coffee Rowan sipped at it and looked around her at the café's interior. It was filled with the sound of clinking china and animated voices. Everyone seemed to be using it as a refuge from the rain. She felt very content. It was good to sit there in the dry, drinking a decent cup of coffee and chatting with someone warm, friendly and interesting.

The talk between them moved on to the subject of Hal and his writing. Rowan spoke of his new novel that was due for publication in the autumn, after which Alison said how

impressed she had been with *Spectre at the Feast*. Rowan told
her then, with pride, of the big movie deal that had transpired
and of Hal's contract for the screenplay, which he was soon
due to start work on. 'He's just waiting for the producer to
get over from Hollywood,' she said, ' – then they'll discuss it
all and he'll have to get busy. In a way I think he's a little afraid
of it – not having tackled such a thing before. But he can do it,
though – of course he can.'

'Is he working on anything at the moment?'

Rowan nodded. 'A novel.'

'And how's it going?'

'Oh – well – I'm afraid the move rather got in the way – of
everything. He's only just getting back to it now.' She smiled.
'He'll be all right once he's really got going again, though. And
at least he's got the perfect place to work in. All the peace and
quiet anyone could need. I really don't know how he managed
before.'

'Obviously you're very happy here,' Alison said, looking at
her with a level gaze.

'Oh, yes, I love it.'

'You have a beautiful house – the old Crispin place. It has so
much character.'

'And space,' Rowan added quickly, 'which we're not at all
used to. Not to mention a whole acre of land.' She grinned.
'A whole acre. We even have a gardener, can you believe that?'

'What's his name?'

'Tom Freeman. He was recommended to us by Paul Cassen
– the doctor.'

'Oh, I know Paul Cassen.'

'We hesitated about taking him on at first – the old man –
Tom Freeman,' Rowan said. 'I mean, he is getting on a bit. But
he's a marvellous old chap, and he seems very fit and active for
his age – apart from which he was so keen to have the job. And
he does seem to know what he's doing.'

'It helps,' Alison said. 'And what about your housekeeper? Is
she from the village?'

'Oh, no, she came with us from London.' She turned

and peered from the window, looking for some sign of Mrs Prescot. 'Oh, good,' she said, 'the rain has stopped . . .'

Alison followed her glance onto the street, where the pedestrians were beginning to make their appearance again. 'I think I'd better take the opportunity and go while I can,' she said.

'Oh, must you? Stay for another cup of coffee.'

'No, I'd better not – just in case Miss Carroll's waiting for her books.' She opened her purse and began to sort through coins. 'No,' Rowan said, 'I'll take care of it.' Alison smiled and nodded. 'Thank you. Next time it's on me.' She was gathering up her lighter and cigarettes and putting them into her bag.

'I hope there will be a next time,' Rowan said.

'Yes, I hope so too.' Alison smiled at her warmly. 'It was really nice to meet you, and talk to you. It would be nice if we could do it again – sometime when I don't have to rush off.'

'You must come to the house and meet Hal.'

'I'd enjoy that, very much.'

They exchanged telephone numbers then, after which Alison got up and put on her coat. With a final smiling farewell she went away. From the window Rowan watched as she hurried off along the street. Her feeling of contentment had grown. Added to the other joys of living in Moorstone she had now found a friend.

'Good morning, Rowan . . .'

She turned at the sound of the voice and saw Paul Cassen standing at the table smiling down at her. An elderly woman was at his side.

'Oh, hello, Paul.' Rowan returned his smile.

'This is a bit of luck,' he went on. 'I came in here and saw Mrs Palfrey and then caught sight of you as well. So – I thought it was a good opportunity for the two of you to meet.' His hand moved briefly between them: 'Mrs Palfrey . . . Mrs Graham . . .'

Smiling, but a little puzzled, Rowan got to her feet and shook hands with the woman. Mrs Palfrey appeared to be somewhere in her middle-to-late sixties. She wore a blue raincoat, and on her fine, frizzled grey hair a neat little hat was perched. Her face was thin, with small features. The smile she gave Rowan looked friendly but shy.

'Mrs Palfrey is the lady I was telling Hal about,' Cassen said. Then he must have seen the puzzlement in Rowan's face for he added quickly, ' – Hal told me that your housekeeper is leaving in a week or so and that you'd probably be needing someone else for a while.'

'Oh, that.' Rowan nodded her understanding. 'Oh, yes, he did mention that he'd spoken of it to you. But our plans have changed now. Mrs Prescot's not going just yet after all.'

' – Oh, I see . . .'

'She's agreed now to stay on till the end of May.' She looked from Cassen to the woman. 'And then, you see, I don't think we'll need anyone else. Certainly not full-time, anyway. It's mainly for these first weeks while we're still getting settled, you understand – when there's still so much to do.' She paused; shrugged. 'We reckoned another month ought to do it – and Mrs Prescot kindly agreed.'

Cassen nodded. 'I see. I wasn't aware that the situation had changed.'

'It was only decided last night.'

'Ah . . .' He turned then to the elderly woman at his side. 'I'm afraid, Mrs Palfrey,' he said with a sympathetic little smile, 'it looks as if I've been a bit too quick off the mark.'

She looked up at him and then at Rowan. 'Oh, well, never mind.' To Rowan she gave her shy little smile. 'Anyway, I'm pleased for you that you've got it all – sorted out. And it's been very nice to meet you.'

Rowan smiled back. 'And you . . .'

There was a little awkward hesitation and then, nodding her farewells, Mrs Palfrey edged away and moved to her own table some little distance across the room. Rowan watched her as she sat down, and then resumed her own seat. Cassen sat on the edge of the chair facing her. 'I'm sorry about that,' he said. 'I hope I didn't put you in an embarrassing spot.'

'Oh, no, not at all. Please don't apologize.' She paused.

'Anyway, if we do decide we still need some help after Mrs Prescot's gone then we can always think about it again.'

'That would be appreciated . . .'

The waitress came to the table then and asked Cassen if he wanted to order. No, he told her, he was just leaving. When she had gone he got up from his chair, glanced briefly over at Mrs Palfrey and said: 'Yes, do think about her, won't you – when your housekeeper's gone?'

'Yes, of course.' Rowan observed Mrs Palfrey for a moment, watching as she lifted her coffee cup to her mouth. The woman didn't look particularly robust, she thought. And her hands – she hadn't noticed them before, but she did now – and she saw that they were rather misshapen, the fingers somewhat twisted and the knuckles enlarged. 'Does she suffer from arthritis?' she quietly asked.

'Yes, I'm afraid she does. Not nearly as much as she used to, though. And anyway, it doesn't hamper her in the slightest.' He looked at Rowan for a moment then gave her a wide smile. 'Well, I'd better get back to work.' He lightly touched his hand to her shoulder, said goodbye and went away. Seconds later she saw him go by on the shining wet pavement. Almost at the same moment Mrs Prescot came into view and Rowan turned to the door and waved to her as she entered. Mrs Prescot gave a little wave of acknowledgement, deposited her umbrella in the stand and came over to join Rowan at the table. 'Sorry I've been such a long time,' she said. 'What with the queues and the rain I thought I'd never get here.'

Rowan ordered coffees and Danish pastries. Fifteen minutes later when they got up to go Mrs Prescot said: 'When we get back I must give Kathleen a ring and tell her I'll be staying on a while longer.' Rowan nodded and glanced towards the table at which Mrs Palfrey had been sitting. She was no longer there.

At the cash register Rowan paid the bill and took up her umbrella. As she hitched her bag more securely under her arm she turned and saw Mrs Prescot looking in dismay at the umbrella stand.

'What's up?' Rowan asked.

Mrs Prescot lifted out the two umbrellas that stood there, looked contemptuously at them for a moment and then put them back again.

'Neither one is mine,' she said. She shook her head in annoyance. 'Would you believe it? Someone's gone off with my umbrella by mistake!'

6

Kathleen Fields turned off the gas under the small saucepan and poured the hot chocolate into the mug. After switching off the kitchen light she carried the mug into the sitting room and sat down again in front of the television set. *News at Ten* was about to come on. When a lull occurred in the sound she heard, faintly from above, the murmur of Mr Simpkins's television. Obviously he was watching a different channel. He was a pleasant man, she reflected – as was the other tenant, Mr Ferreira. They both paid their rent regularly and kept their rooms neat. And so what if Mr Simpkins did sometimes have a drop too much on the occasional Friday night? – he never got boisterous with it.

She sipped from the steaming mug. Why was it, she idly wondered, that hot chocolate should have that touch of luxury about it? It always had done for her. And for Elsie too, for that matter. When Elsie was there the regular nightly cup of cocoa was a part of the ritual of their shared lives. They always enjoyed it so much. It tasted good now, too – but it wasn't quite the same without Elsie there.

Kathleen wore a floral print dressing gown. It was another part of her pursuit of comfort to relax like this for the last hour before going to bed. And it was particularly comforting if her day at the office had been more than usually tiring. Still, the possibility of such days occurring wouldn't last much longer. Another six months and she'd be retiring – on a well-earned pension after her years of service in a minor department of a local government office.

For the moment, though, she was looking forward to Elsie's return. Unlike her sister, Kathleen had never married, and after her years of aloneness the closeness of her younger sister had grown increasingly important to her.

Up until some ten years ago the two had led separate lives, Kathleen putting her energies into her job and the comfort of her paying guests, and Elsie totally involved with her family – a husband and son. And then that son, Norman, whilst still a student, had been killed in a motoring accident abroad. That, a most terrible time, had brought the two sisters closer. Then, when Elsie's husband had died quietly in a hospital bed the closeness had grown stronger still. From then on the lives of the two women had been spent together.

Until recently, that is, when Elsie had decided to go down to Devon to help her nice young couple, the Grahams, get settled in. She hadn't been that keen to go, Kathleen knew, but the Grahams had been so good to her in the past, and what with losing their little boy like that and everything, well – Elsie just hadn't been able to say no once the suggestion was made.

And now she'd phoned to say that she'd decided to stay on for another month. Kathleen sighed her disappointment. Still, she told herself, a month wasn't forever, and the time would soon pass. And anyway, it was a good experience for Elsie; she'd never lived in the country before.

Idly, Kathleen wondered what they should do once she had retired. Perhaps they should sell the house and move somewhere else. Find something smaller, with just enough room for the two of them. Perhaps some nice little semi in the suburbs where there'd be a bit of garden. That would be nice. . . .

Before her the television news reader was quoting the Prime Minister's latest comments on the state of the country's economy. Kathleen shook her head, got up, switched off the set and sat back again on the sofa. Sipping at her chocolate she eagerly took up the threads of her earlier thoughts.

The garden; a garden, yes . . .

One thing she was determined on and that was that she'd keep active once she'd given up work at the office. Too many people, she often said, just seemed to give in once there were no longer demands made of them. Not she. She looked forward to having more free time – and looked forward to using it. After all, she was fit and healthy; she'd hardly ever had a day's illness in her life. Retirement for her wouldn't mean an end to anything; on the contrary, it could be – it would be – a beginning.

The smile that came with the comforting thought stayed on her lips for a moment longer before it was wiped out by the ugly grimace that widened her eyes and stretched her mouth in a silent scream.

As the stabbing pain screwed into her heart she gasped in agony, snatching at her breath, letting fall the mug so that the remains of the chocolate splattered her dressing gown and the cushions of the sofa. With her face distorted she half rose to her feet, standing with knees bent, left hand clutched to her chest and the other reaching out to the empty room for help.

As her breath returned and the pain increased she cried out, 'God – oh, God! Oh, God – help me – !'

She was a tall woman and as she crashed sideways she caught the small table with her shoulder and sent that over too.

As she lay there the only sounds to be heard were her harsh breathing and the faint, continuing murmur of Mr Simpkins's television on the floor above.

7

As Hal entered the kitchen just on six-thirty he found Rowan preparing the dinner. No, she told him, she didn't need any help. He had just poured a drink for each of them when the phone rang. Rowan answered it. It was Mrs Prescot. Minutes later he watched as Rowan hung up the receiver, sighed and sadly shook her head.

'How is Kathleen?' he asked.

'Not so good, I'm afraid.'

'What does Mrs Prescot say it was?'

'A heart attack. And a pretty massive one, it seems. Thank God the tenant found her when he did. As it is she's in a pretty bad way.'

'Oh, God,' Hal groaned. 'Do they think she'll recover?'

Rowan shrugged. 'Who knows. If she does her life from now on will be very different; very limited. Oh, it's so sad. And the way Mrs Prescot would talk of her she always seemed such a healthy woman.'

'And how is she – Mrs Prescot?'

'Very upset – very shaken, naturally.' She paused. 'She won't be coming back here now, of course.'

'No . . .' Hal had realized that when he'd taken Mrs Prescot to the station early that morning, soon after she'd got the news. He had known then that she was leaving Moorstone for good. Now, with her telephone call she had only confirmed his belief.

After a few more minutes, during which they discussed Kathleen's illness and its ramifications, Rowan said: 'And as for us – well, it only gets things moving a bit faster, doesn't it? I mean, we knew she'd be leaving sometime. It's just happened a lot sooner and more suddenly than we'd expected.' She shrugged. 'But I daresay we shall manage perfectly well on our own.'

'No.' Hal shook his head. 'Be sensible now. We can afford some help around the house, so why not have it? There's a lot to do around here and if you try to do it all on your own you'll never do anything else. What about your own writing? Your stories? I thought you were keen to get back to that.'

'I am.'

'Good. Then in that case you must have help. Particularly at a time like this when we're still finding our way and getting things the way we want them.'

'But – I just don't know that I want any – stranger here – not after Mrs Prescot.'

'Oh, I know what you mean, all right. That's the way I feel. But – well, it's either we do or you make a career of house-work.'

'I suppose you're right.'

He nodded. 'Good. That's settled then. We'll start looking around for someone. – Not to live in, but just to come in part-time. That would be best, wouldn't it? – Three or four days a week – like Tom Freeman . . .'

'Yes, that would be fine.'

He was silent for a moment then said, 'I suppose we could put an ad in one of the papers.'

'Mmm . . .' Rowan nodded doubtfully, then: 'What about Paul Cassen's friend – Mrs Palfrey? I did promise we'd give her consideration before anybody else . . .'

Hal wasn't enthusiastic. 'By the way you described her,' he said, 'she doesn't strike me as being the most . . . suitable. We don't want someone who's going to be more of a liability than a help.'

Rowan nodded agreement. 'True . . . though Paul did say that she was very capable.'

Before Hal could say anything to this there was a ring at the doorbell. He went into the hall, opened the door and saw Paul Cassen standing there.

'Am I calling at a bad time?' Cassen said. He eyed Hal keenly. 'I've just been to see one of your neighbours and I thought I'd drop in on you for a minute before I go home.'

'You called at a very *good* time.' Hal stood back, opening the door wider. 'We're just having a drink. Come and join us.'

'Are you sure it's not inconvenient?'

'Of course not.'

He led Cassen into the sitting room, where he called out to Rowan that they had a guest and then poured the doctor a vodka and tonic. Rowan entered carrying their own drinks. 'I won't stay long,' Cassen said to her. 'I have to get back for dinner soon.'

'As a matter of fact,' Rowan said, 'we had just that minute mentioned your name . . .'

'Oh . . . ?'

'We were discussing your friend Mrs Palfrey.' She paused; sighed. 'Our Mrs Prescot's gone back to London.'

Cassen frowned. After a moment he said, 'When did that happen?'

'This morning. Hal drove her into Exeter and she got the train.'

Another pause before Cassen spoke again. 'Is – is she all right?' he asked.

'Yes, of course – she's fine. Why shouldn't she be? Her sister isn't, though. She's been taken ill with a heart attack. Quite a severe one.'

'Oh, dear, how sad.' Cassen gave a shake of his head. 'When was that – that her sister was taken ill?'

'Last night, so it would appear. She wasn't found till this morning. One of her tenants found her and phoned Mrs Prescot here . . .'

'And it's serious, you say . . .'

'Yes.' Rowan gave a shrug. 'So – Mrs Prescot's gone back to be with her – and take care of her.'

'So she won't be coming back . . .'

'No, I'm afraid not.' She sighed. 'We shall really miss her.'

'I'm sure you will.' Cassen paused for a moment, then said: 'And were you thinking of giving Mrs Palfrey a try – now that Mrs Prescot's gone?'

Rowan glanced briefly at Hal before she answered. 'Well, actually, Hal's not too keen on the idea . . . We were thinking of advertising . . .'

'I see.' Cassen nodded. Then, turning to Hal, he said, 'May I ask why, Hal – why you're not too keen?'

Hal shrugged. 'I'm only judging on what Ro's told me,' he said awkwardly. 'And going by that I just – have doubts that Mrs Palfrey's the right one. I mean going by her description she seems to be a bit on the – the frail side . . .'

'Oh, she's not frail,' Cassen said. 'She might look it, but she's not. She's a wiry little thing – and very capable. Why don't you give her a try? See how it works out . . . ?'

'Are you getting a commission?' Hal asked with a grin.

'A commission – ?'

'Well, you've already supplied us with our gardener – and

now it's the domestic help.' He chuckled. 'You're getting a cut of their salaries, aren't you?'

Cassen laughed along with him. 'So you've guessed! No, but seriously, I'm only trying to give a deserving woman a helping hand – and help you two at the same time. You need someone, and she's a very sweet lady who needs a job – and, further, would be an asset.'

'She gets her pension, doesn't she?' Hal asked.

'Oh, yes, of course. But she doesn't like to just sit back. She thrives on keeping busy.' He paused. 'Think about it – why don't you?'

Rowan looked over at Hal. 'What do you think . . . ?'

Before Hal could reply, Cassen said, 'I should also say that she's most reliable – and completely trustworthy.'

'Isn't everyone in Moorstone?' Hal said, smiling. Then he shrugged and turned to Rowan. 'Well . . . I'll leave it to you, Ro.'

She looked from one man to the other. 'I suppose we could give it a try, couldn't we? See how she works out . . . ?'

Cassen smiled his satisfaction. 'Good, good. I'm so pleased. I'm sure you'll both be very glad. Shall I mention it to her, then?'

Rowan nodded. 'Yes, why not?' Then she added, 'Of course, she might decide she doesn't want to come and work for us.'

Cassen brushed this idea aside with a wave of his hand. 'Right,' he said, 'I'll tell her to get in touch with you. When – Monday morning?'

'Might as well,' Rowan said. 'We don't plan on going any-where.'

'Fine.'

With the business of Mrs Palfrey settled for the moment, the talk moved on to other things. Cassen, looking around him, said how attractive the room was looking, and how well their own furniture co-ordinated with the old pieces they'd taken along with the house. After that he went on to ask Hal how the new novel was progressing. Hal, lying, replied that it was going well. . . .

'Have you met our other resident writer?' Cassen asked.

'Edith Carroll? No, not yet. Rowan mentioned her to me.'

'I haven't met her, though,' Rowan said quickly. 'I just happened to bump into her secretary – Alison Lucas. She told me a little about her.'

Cassen nodded. 'Oh, yes, I know Alison. A very nice girl. Of course,' he went on, turning back to Hal, 'Edith Carroll doesn't write the kind of things you write. And I don't think she writes nearly as quickly as you do, either. From what I gather, it takes her two or three years to do a book. And she's getting on a bit now, so she's slower than she was.'

'I must read something of hers,' Hal said. 'I'll see what there is in the library.'

'You should,' Cassen said. 'She writes well.'

'Moorstone seems to hold an attraction for writers,' Hal said.

'No . . .' Cassen shook his head. 'It attracts all kinds – people in all kinds of professions.' He grinned. 'Even accountants aren't immune.'

'What do you mean?' Rowan asked.

'That's what I was – when I first came here.'

'Oh, really? And how was that? How did you come here?'

'I was on a motoring holiday. I'd just intended to take a break for a few days – to get away on my own. Like you two I was based in London.' He smiled. 'And – I just – came across the village.'

'And how did you come to stay here?'

He was silent for a moment, as if looking back into the past. 'As I remember, I started off by deciding to stay on for a few weeks. I had some leave owing to me – and with the relationship I had going with my wife there was nothing in London I felt like hurrying back for. And I really liked this place. I loved it – and it seemed to me to be the perfect spot for getting away from it all.' He grinned. 'Sounds corny, doesn't it? But I was very dissatisfied and mixed up about my life, I can tell you. Apart from my marriage being a disaster I was also very unhappy with my job. I didn't know what to do about anything. Anyway, one day when I was in the bar at The Swan – I had a room there – I got talking to one of the locals – a doctor – John Richmond. He told me that his assistant had recently left – and the next thing he was offering me the job. It wasn't much of one, I'll admit – just doing his bookkeeping and bits of clerical work – answering the phone and so on. But I was glad of it; I jumped at it. Because – well, I wanted to stay on for a while.'

'And so that was it,' Hal said.

'That was it.' Cassen nodded. 'I left The Swan and took a room at Dr Richmond's house.'

'Does he still live here?' Rowan asked.

'No – I'm afraid he's dead now. He died only a few weeks after I moved in.' Cassen looked thoughtfully into the distance. 'He was the most fantastic person. And like a father to me.' He paused. 'Can you imagine? – I'd only known him a little while, but when he died I found that he'd left me everything. Everything he had.'

'My God,' Rowan breathed, 'that's incredible.'

'Isn't it? And it was that that enabled me to take up medicine. It was his money and it was his influence – of course. And I was young enough. And I studied hard – and when I qualified I came back here. I was divorced from Marianne by then – and I married Sandra. Sandra lived in the village. She was one of the reasons I came back here – apart from loving the place – and feeling that I owed it something.' He smiled. 'So there you have it. And Moorstone really is my home now.' He looked from one to the other. 'And now it's your home too. And believe me, it's a good place to be.'

'That's what I feel,' Rowan said. 'I've felt it all along.'

Cassen nodded. 'It's the way nearly everyone feels. Even those who've lived here and then have to leave for some reason or other. I know I felt like that when I went away to study. I couldn't wait to get back. And other people – they go away for years and years – but they always return, it seems – always. At least they always intend to. Like Childs, for example. He'd always planned to return.'

'The previous owner of this house,' Rowan said.

Cassen smiled. 'There's only one Lewis Childs.'

'I've been wondering about him,' Hal said. 'I think I've heard about him in some other connection – apart from his having been the owner of this place.'

'You might well have done,' said Cassen. 'He's made the newspapers on a few occasions.'

'That's right.' Hal nodded. 'That's why his name rang a bell when we bought this house. I must have read something about him.'

Rowan, shaking her head, said, 'How could someone own a place like this – this house – and then sell it? I couldn't.'

'Oh, he never did live in this house,' Cassen answered. 'This house was left to him by one of the villagers. He's got his own place in the village – though he hasn't set foot in the place for ages.'

'It's coming back to me now,' Hal said thoughtfully. 'Isn't he one of the – jet-setting crowd?'

'That's right.'

'Yes . . . It's hard to imagine him being associated with this place – as coming from this little village. He's something of a playboy, isn't he?'

'Yes, I suppose you'd call him something of an adventurer.' Cassen shook his head. 'Though with all his wild and wonderful experiences and his endless travelling around he always kept his house ready for his return. He always intended to come back some day.'

'You're talking of him now in the past tense,' Rowan said. 'Has he changed his mind? Has he decided now not to return?'

Cassen hesitated before he answered. 'I don't think he's at all likely to be going anywhere now,' he said. 'Not after that accident.'

'What accident was that?' Hal asked.

'I thought you might have read about it. It was mentioned in some of the papers. I don't know any of the details, but he was hurt very badly. A car crash, apparently. A week or so ago. By what I've been told his chances of recovery are very slim. Last thing I heard he was still in a coma.'

'That's sad,' Rowan said. 'So he'll never come back to his house now.' She turned in her chair to look out onto the garden where the birds filled the peace of the evening with their song. After a moment she murmured, 'Moorstone is the kind of place I'd want to return to – to rest. Though I don't think I'd ever want to leave here in the first place.'

Cassen looked at her, gently smiling. Then, glancing at his watch he gave a sigh and said: 'Well, Sandra will be wondering where I am. And I must let you two get on with your dinner.' He swallowed the last of his drink, put down his glass and got up. 'So,' he said as he preceded the two of them into the hall, ' – I'll have a word with Mrs Palfrey and get her to give you a ring.'

'Fine,' Rowan said.

He was just moving to the front door when Rowan added quickly, 'Oh, Paul, just wait a moment, will you?'

'Of course.'

She turned and stepped across the hall into the room that had been Mrs Prescot's. When she reappeared a few seconds later she held in her hand one of the umbrellas that had been left in the stand at the café.

'I just wondered,' she said, 'whether there was a chance that you might know who this belongs to. – You know most of the villagers . . .'

'No.' Cassen shook his head. 'I haven't a clue. Why?'

'When Mrs Prescot and I were in the café yesterday morning someone took her umbrella and left this one in its place. There was this one and another one in the stand when we were leaving. The other one was claimed by someone there when the manageress made enquiries, but – not this one. The thing is, the one that was taken didn't even belong to Mrs Prescot. It was her sister's.'

'Ah,' said Cassen, ' – it was her sister's. – The one who's just been taken ill . . .'

'Yes.' Rowan nodded. 'So of course I'd like to get it back and return it to her.' She sighed. 'Not that it seems she'll have that much use for it – not now.'

8

When Mrs Palfrey switched off the vacuum cleaner she could hear again the sound of Rowan's typewriter from her little study on the left of the hall. Next to it was the room that Mrs Prescot had occupied – a neat little bed-sitter with its own television set. Not that Mrs Palfrey would be needing a room here; like Tom Freeman in the garden she was only employed part-time – on Mondays, Tuesdays, Wednesdays and Fridays. Four days, the Grahams had decided, would be enough.

Mrs Palfrey looked at her little gold watch. Just after ten-thirty. She'd finish doing the hall carpet, polish the banister rail and then make a start upstairs. Then it would be time to begin preparing lunch. Today, Monday, was her first day in Crispin's House. Earlier this morning she had telephoned the Grahams and then come round to see them. The interview hadn't taken long and at the end of it she'd been hired for a trial period of a month, starting – at her own suggestion – immediately. Only one month. Mr Graham hadn't been 'exactly sure' what their future plans were, he'd told her. But she knew better; she wasn't fooled. He wasn't sure of her, that's what it was. She could tell; he hadn't been at all convinced that she'd be suitable. She'd prove him wrong, though, wait and see.

She did her work thoroughly as she went about her various tasks. She wasn't going to be one of those brooms that swept clean only because it was new. Now that she'd got the job she was determined to keep it for as long as she chose – for as long as it suited her. The month she'd been given *should* be enough – but just in case . . .

She pushed the Hoover across the carpet. Cleaning, cooking, looking after someone else's house – it wasn't the job for her, and, there was no doubt, she was getting too old for it. But for the moment it was necessary, and she would cope with all its demands. . . .

Because of the noise of the cleaner she didn't hear the door open. But then, turning, she saw Rowan standing in the open doorway of her study. Mrs Palfrey depressed the stop button with her foot and turned to her, smiling.

'I've just about finished here, Mrs Graham,' she said. 'I thought then that before getting the lunch I'd make a start upstairs if there's time.'

Rowan nodded. 'Fine . . .'

Rowan's smile was very warm, very friendly. Mrs Palfrey studied her; a quick, brief assessment as she stood before her; not for the first time and not for the last. She looked admiringly at the slim figure, the thick, dark hair, the graceful oval of the face and the slender-fingered hands. She was beautiful.

'I'm just about to make some coffee,' Rowan said. 'We always have some about this time. Would you like a cup?'

Mrs Palfrey shook her head. 'Thank you, but I don't think so – not right now. But let me make it –'

'No, I can do it.'

'No, please, let me. It won't take me a minute and you and Mr Graham have more important things to do.'

'Oh, well . . . okay . . .'

Alone in the kitchen a few moments later Mrs Palfrey put on the kettle and carefully measured the ground coffee into the filter. While the water was heating she set out trays on which she placed cups and saucers, and plates holding a few assorted biscuits. When the coffee was ready she took one tray into Rowan's study and the other upstairs. There she knocked on Hal's door and on hearing his answering call went in and found him sitting idly at his desk. His typewriter, she noticed, was covered; nothing much seemed to be happening – except that he was smoking too heavily; the ashtray was almost overflowing. Setting the tray down, she nodded a silent, smiling acknowledgement of his thanks and went back downstairs to the hall.

When her work was finished there she picked up the vacuum cleaner and carried it up the stairs. It was heavy. Still, she consoled herself, it had to be done and soon she would have her reward. And anyway, the job wasn't going to last forever.

In the bathroom at the far end of the house she cleaned the bathtub and then started on the hand basin. In the middle of her work she stopped and looked down at her hands – misshapen, aging, mottled now with brown spots. Raising her head she gazed at her reflection in the glass, taking in the dull, frizzled hair, the snub nose and the wrinkles in the dry skin. It had never, even when young, been a pretty face. She sighed, and went back to polishing the taps.

Finished at last she glanced down from the window and saw that Rowan had left her study and was now standing outside talking to Tom Freeman. He stood with one hand on his spade, his grey head nodding occasionally as he spoke and gestured. A slight breeze ruffled Rowan's dark hair, blowing it across her cheek.

Mrs Palfrey looked away and critically eyed the results of her efforts. The taps over the bathtub and the basin were gleaming. Surely that Mrs Prescot couldn't have done any better – if she could have done as well.

That was a funny business, she thought, that thing with the past housekeeper. Who'd have guessed that the umbrella would turn out to be her sister's? Still, the outcome of it all had been the right one. Mrs Prescot had gone and now here was she, Mrs Palfrey, in her place. And that was all that mattered.

A little later she put on her kitchen gloves and went out into the garden. She walked past the laburnum tree and on along the path to where Tom Freeman was tending the large vegetable patch. At her request he picked a lettuce and filled her basket with runner beans. She nodded approvingly. 'And I'll need some rosemary and mint – ' she said, ' – and a few other things . . .'

He looked at her for a moment and then gestured off. 'Over there.' He turned and led the way from the vegetable patch to a spot near the orchard where the wild flowers and shrubs grew unchecked. Here were rosemary, thyme, mint and all kinds of fragrant herbs. Here, too, among the brambles in the lower areas the deadly spurge laurel's sweet-scented flowers grew as high as Mrs Palfrey's waist while the bittersweet's blossoms reached taller than her head.

The old man stood watching as she moved about, bending low, stretching high, gathering what she needed. When she was done he led her to the rose garden where he cut a dozen of the finest blooms. 'They'll make a beautiful centrepiece,' she said, bending her little snub nose to the scent. Straightening again, she said, 'You know – I just realized – it's May Day.' She smiled. 'It's a time of beginning. . . .' She stood there for a moment, then her smile faded and she gave a little sigh. 'Ah, well,' she said, ' – I suppose I must go and start preparing lunch.'

Tom Freeman walked with her along the path. When they reached the vegetable patch they stopped. She shifted the weight of the basket to her other hand and he eyed her keenly for a moment then said:

'You think you'll manage?'

'Of course I will. I've got no choice.' She paused. 'And you?' He was looking tired, she thought; a little grey-faced. And it was early days yet.

With a grimace he stretched slightly, as if easing an ache in his back. 'Like you,' he said, 'it's a case of having to. Still – knowing it's in sight makes it a lot easier.'

Putting her free hand down into the basket she moved aside the roses. There next to the beans and the lettuce lay the bits of leaves and flowers she had gathered by the orchard. She nodded. 'Oh, yes, we'll manage all right.' When she raised her head again and looked into the old man's eyes her mouth was curved in the smallest of smiles. 'And hopefully,' she added, 'it won't have to be for very long.'

'Are you going to start today?' he asked. There was a trace of eagerness in his voice.

'No, tomorrow. They've got a visitor this evening. Tomorrow will be soon enough.'

'And it will be for *both* of them, won't it?'

She pretended to think about it for a moment, pursing her lips and frowning. She enjoyed the look of increasing anxiety on his face. Then, 'Yes,' she said at last. 'Of course.'

'Thank you.' He looked relieved. After a second or two he said: 'What do you think of them?'

'Perfect. If appearances are anything to go by.' She tapped the side of the basket. 'Anyway, once I've had a chance to use this stuff we should know.'

'You won't overdo it, will you?'

Briefly, in disdain, she lowered her eyelids. 'Please – credit me with some intelligence. I *have* done it before.' She'd never cared for him. 'If you can think of a better way of getting them there – and getting what's needed – then you're welcome to try.'

'No, no,' he said, shaking his head. 'You do what you think is best.' He looked sheepish. As if trying to regain firmer ground he asked, 'Who've they got coming this evening, then?'

'Edith Carroll's girl – Alison Lucas. She's coming to dinner.'

'Oh, yes, the Lucas girl. How's she getting on there?'

'Fine, I believe.'

'She's taking her time, isn't she – Edith Carroll?'

'I suppose she is, rather. But she says she's got work to finish.'

'I don't see that that makes any difference.'

'Neither do I, but there's no accounting for some people's actions.'

'Well, I don't intend to wait,' he said, ' – any longer than I have to.'

'Quite.' She gave a little shake of her head. 'And the way I'm feeling it can't come soon enough.'

'It's silly to wait,' he said. 'Things can go wrong. Anything could happen. You can end up with sweet bugger all.'

'Just try to remember that you're talking to a lady, will you?' she said curtly. Then, pleased with his contrite expression she added:

'But don't worry. Nothing will go wrong.'

9

They had lingered through dinner and when at last it was over had moved into the sitting room where Hal served coffee. He was enjoying Alison's company. She had a bright, warm personality and nice sense of humour. Furthermore she possessed a down-to-earth common sense that was both welcome and refreshing – qualities, he suddenly realized, that he had missed since coming to Moorstone. In addition, the fact that she herself was a relative newcomer to the village was also a mark in her favour. He was pleased, very pleased, that Rowan had found in her a friend. He looked over at Rowan as she sat stirring her coffee. She looked happy and relaxed.

Now, to increase his pleasure in the evening, he discovered that Alison shared, to a degree, his own love of music of the forties. Having set down her own cup she was carefully browsing through his collection of old seventy-eights.

'One of Hal's passions,' Rowan told her.

Alison smiled. 'I approve of such passions.' Turning to Hal she asked: 'Please – play me something, will you?'

He was delighted to comply. Most of the records in his collection had been made before he was born – the rest before he had been aware of any musical sense. He had started gathering them by stumbling on a couple of rare items whilst still in his teens; and the bug had bitten. By this time, after many years, his collection had grown considerably; now it took up three four-foot-long shelves. All those heavy old singles, coming from a time when each one had been something of an event possessed – in their romance, their specialness – a charm for him that today's records, turned out in their millions, could never have.

> I get along without you very well,
> Of course I do . . .

While the plaintive voice of Billie Holiday filled the room he lit a cigarette and stood gazing out onto the darkened garden. When the record came to an end he took it off and, fingertips brushing the polished wood of the cabinet, said, 'This is the perfect machine for these old records.' To Alison he added: 'We got it with the house. We were lucky there.'

'We were lucky with everything,' Rowan said. 'This house and this village.' Turning, smiling, toward Alison she asked, 'Don't you just love it here?'

To Hal's ears Alison's answer of 'Yes . . .' didn't sound too convincing. 'You don't seem that sure,' he said.

She shrugged. 'Oh, it's all right, I suppose. But it's – well, it's not really my cup of tea.'

Rowan looked at her in surprise. 'Are you serious? What is it about it that you're not keen on? I mean – it's got everything that a small English village should have. This place is story-book stuff. Loads of charm, beautiful scenery, a sense of community – and the people couldn't be nicer.'

'Ah, yes, the people,' Alison said. 'Sometimes I think they're a little *too* nice.'

'I don't understand,' said Rowan. There was a touch of dismay in her expression. 'The people here are pleasant – but surely it's typical of the difference between people in the country and in the city.' She gave a defiant little laugh. 'Believe me, after London I find it a very refreshing change. I wouldn't have it any other way.'

Alison looked at her for a moment, nodded, then said: 'Yes, maybe you're right. After all, why shouldn't people be nice to each other? Yes, I suppose that when you come to think about it it's less an indictment of the people here in the village than of those outside it.'

'What made you choose Moorstone in the first place?' Hal asked. 'How did you find it?'

'I answered an ad in *The Times*. After Geoff went off I got to feeling very much at a loose end; I was between jobs and I just – just wanted to get away somewhere. So, as I say, I answered the ad – Miss Carroll's – came down to meet her – and got the job.' She grinned. 'Sometimes when I think of the competition there was for it I can't understand why she came to choose me. I mean, let's be honest – my typing's okay, but it's not about to win me any medals. And I didn't get beyond lesson three in my shorthand course. Not like some of those other women who applied. I came across some of the letters from them – applying for the job. My God, some of them sounded absolutely brilliant. Still,' she shrugged, 'I've managed all right, and there haven't been any complaints – so far.'

Hal asked her then whether she found the work interesting. 'Yes, I do,' she answered, 'but there – the business of creative writing has always fascinated me.'

'Do you write, yourself?'

'Oh, no.' She shook her head. 'I've no talent whatsoever in that direction. It's as much as I can manage to write a letter. No – I just have a great respect for those who can do it – and can do it well. But I know at the same time that I could never do it myself. And I don't have the slightest desire to try, either.' She smiled. 'It's funny; Miss Carroll's often suggested to me that I try my hand at writing something. Maybe a short story – something like that. It's no good, though. I just tell her politely that she's wasting her breath.'

While Rowan poured more coffee Hal offered Alison a cigarette. When it was alight she said, 'That's the only thing I have against Miss Carroll as my employer: she won't let me smoke – except in my room. And I know she only tolerates that with the greatest difficulty. I suppose she puts up with it to keep me happy. She absolutely hates it. Still – ' she shrugged, ' – I suppose we're none of us perfect. But even Ralph Collins isn't allowed to smoke in her presence. And she idolizes him – though God knows why.'

Hal grinned. 'Collins – from the library. He's your admirer, isn't he? Rowan was telling me something about it . . .'

'I'm sorry I mentioned his name.' Alison gave a mock shudder. 'Please – let's not spoil a lovely evening talking about that loathsome creature. Let's talk about other things . . .'

They did, and the talk went on until almost eleven-thirty, at which time Alison said she really would have to get going. As she got up Hal said he'd take her back in the car. No, she said, thanking him, it was kind of him but it was no distance. '. . . and besides,' she added, 'I'd quite like to walk.'

'Then I'll walk back with you,' he said, to which Rowan added, 'Take your bike – then you can ride it home. I'll get cleared up while you're gone.'

When the two girls had fondly said their goodnights to one another Hal and Alison stepped out into the cool, moon-lit night. Looking up, Hal saw that the sky was clear; all the stars were there. 'It's a beautiful night,' he said. He took his bicycle from the garage and, pushing it beside him, walked with Alison onto the road. Their steps sounded sharp in the stillness. Alison said, 'I had a really nice time, Hal. Thank you so much.'

'Oh, it was our pleasure.' He meant it.

After a few moments had gone by he said: 'What did you mean about the people here being *too nice*?'

'Oh, *that*. Take no notice. That's just my big mouth. I'm sorry I said it.'

'Why be sorry?'

'Well – I shall be leaving Moorstone eventually, whereas you're staying. It just wasn't – tactful of me to be – negative about it. Particularly when Rowan's so obviously in love with the place.'

'Oh, she's sold on it, all right. Completely.'

On either side of them the fields, trees and hedgerows were touched with silver. Up ahead only the occasional lighted windows showed in the clustered houses of the village. 'Anyway, she's right,' Alison said. 'It's a very beautiful little place.'

'It's not everything, though, is it? Beauty . . .' He was looking at her as he spoke and she turned briefly to glance at him. 'A place has got to do more than *look* good,' he added. She said nothing. After a moment he went on: 'I'm interested; I'd really like to know: *why* isn't this place your cup of tea – as you put it?'

'Is it yours?' she asked.

Her question silenced him for a second, then he said: 'Is it the people here? Rowan thinks they're just about perfect.'

'Oh, they're perfect, all right,' she said quickly. 'They're too damn perfect.'

'Go on. . . .'

She paused, then said thoughtfully: 'Well, I think that's it. That's what's wrong – for me, anyway – or one of the things. I find the villagers – to all outward appearances – to be just *too nice*. It reminds me a bit of those freaky Californian religions where everyone goes around being loving and understanding and non-aggressive – and manage to give the impression that they're boiling inside.'

'And is that how you see the people here?'

'Well, not quite like that, but – well, I just don't think it's natural to be that warm and friendly and welcoming. That's the way it strikes me, anyway.' She hesitated for a moment then went on: 'Take last Saturday, for example. I went into the stationer's to get a few things for Miss Carroll and there were two women already there, waiting to be served. And what happens but they stand aside and *insist* that I go first. I found it rather – embarrassing. Dammit, it's not natural to be so bloody . . . sweet. And if one more person asks me whether I'm happy in Moorstone I swear I'll hit him.' She laughed. 'It's almost as if they're afraid that I'm going to get up and leave.'

Hal nodded. 'Yes, I've found that with us, too. Folks being concerned as to whether we're happy here and are settling in all right.'

'And are you? Are you happy here? Are you settling in all right?'

'Rowan is.'

'Yes, I gathered that. What about you?'

'It's all so new for me,' he said non-committally. 'I'm not used to living in the country. I suppose I'll get used to it in time. Anyway, the important thing right now is that Ro's happy. And she *is* happy here. It's made such a difference to her – coming here, having this house . . .'

'Oh, your house is gorgeous.'

'Yes, we love it. And we certainly were lucky there – not only in finding it, but getting it at the price we did.'

'You got a bargain, did you?'

'Yes, I'm sure we did. Mind you, perhaps that's because there was no one else after it. Which, I must say, surprised us . . .'

In the pale light he saw her frown.

'When did you buy it?' she asked.

'Towards the end of February. Why . . . ?'

'Well, it just seems . . . a little odd . . .'

'What do you mean?'

'Well, soon after I got here – before you and Rowan arrived – I got to talking to an elderly couple in The Coffee Shop. They were wanting to move to Moorstone, they told me, and had come that day to look at a house that they'd seen empty. Not that they got it. Anyway, they told me that they'd been disappointed before. Over your house.'

'Oh . . . ?'

'Yes. They'd come to see it back in January, they said.'

'And the price was too high for them, was it?'

'No, apparently not. They told me that the price had been very high but even though they'd been prepared to pay it they'd still been turned down. I felt quite sorry for them. They'd obviously had their hearts set on it, poor old things. Well, it is a lovely place. Mind you, it *ought* to be for that kind of money.'

Slightly puzzled, Hal said: 'You make it sound as if the price was astronomical. It didn't cost very much. Not by today's standards.'

'It depends on what you mean by not very much . . .'

When he told her what he had paid for the house she whistled and said, 'You're joking! Are you serious?'

'Of course.'

'Well, I'll tell you, that wasn't the price quoted to the old couple I talked to. They'd been asked a price way above that. It was at least twenty thousand more. *And* they'd been prepared to pay it, too.'

Hal was silent for a moment, then he said: 'Yes, that is

strange, isn't it?' Then he smiled and shrugged. 'Ah, well, unlucky for them and lucky for us.'

'Your house,' she said after a while, 'it belonged to that character Lewis Childs, didn't it?'

'Oh, you know about him?'

'He's famous. Or infamous. He's often being mentioned in the more salacious gossip columns.'

'I didn't realize he was that well known.'

'You obviously read the wrong papers – or the right ones – whichever way you look at it.'

'Apparently he's in a hospital somewhere on the Continent right now – so Paul Cassen was saying.'

'Yes. Miss Carroll mentioned something about it to me. He's not expected to live, so she said. So he won't be coming back here for his retirement.' When Hal turned to her in surprise she added: 'Haven't they told *you* that? None of the Moorstone people leaves the village forever. Those who go *always* return *eventually*.'

Hal laughed. 'Yes, we've been told the same thing. It's funny – the villagers do seem to have a rather – inordinate degree of loyalty to the place – and pride in it.'

'I'll say they do.'

Going by way of the now silent High Street and School Lane they had walked to the other side of the village. Since starting out they'd seen no sign of anyone else. Now, turning left onto Moorstone Road, Hal saw just a few yards along a large, white-painted Victorian house. 'Well, this is it,' Alison said as they walked towards it. 'The Laurels. My temporary home.'

They came to a stop at the front gate. The upper windows were all dark, but there was a light burning in the hall. 'For my benefit,' Alison whispered. 'They'll have gone to bed ages ago.'

'They?' He kept his own voice very low.

'Yes, there's the housekeeper as well. Miss Allardice.' She paused and then, smiling warmly, added, 'Thanks for walking with me, Hal. I hope I haven't made you late.'

'Oh, no.' He patted the saddle of his bicycle. 'I shall get back in no time at all.'

'Is it new?' she said, 'the bike? It looks it.'

'Yes. We each got one just after we moved in.'

'You're really entering into the spirit of country living.'

He shrugged. 'Making the effort, anyway. Rowan's the one, though. Now she's talking about helping out with jumble sales and joining the village dramatic society. . . .'

'Rather her than me.'

'She believes it's a good way of getting to know the villagers. I'm sure she's right.'

'Oh, I'm sure she is. There certainly isn't much to do here, is there? And one can get tired of looking at pretty views. Of course you could just visit the neighbours, I suppose.'

'Is that what you do?'

'Oh, no. There's nobody here I'd want to call on – until now, that is.' She smiled. 'I had a really super evening, Hal.'

'Good. So did we. And I hope you'll feel like calling on us – often.'

'Thank you. I shall.' Her smile became a wide grin. 'How about that . . . already I feel less . . . isolated.'

Hal frowned. 'Have you felt isolated? That's not so good.'

'It's not, is it? I never considered that when I came here. It never entered my mind. I suppose it's just that I feel rather – tied to the place; for one thing, not having a car here – and I'm not allowed to use Miss Carroll's.'

'But you must have made friends here . . .'

She hesitated before answering. 'I did at the beginning – but I don't know what happened. Still, that's in the past. Now, having met you two, if I can just hold out till Geoff gets back maybe I won't be going to Primrose House after all.'

'Primrose House? What's that?'

Dropping her whispered voice even lower she said, 'Primrose House is the village nuthouse. Didn't you know that?'

'You mean – a mental home . . . ?'

'If you want to be polite, yes, a mental home.'

'Here? In Moorstone?'

'They refer to it as The Old Folks' Home. But I think that's somewhat euphemistic.'

'There's a mental home in a place this size?'

She nodded. 'You obviously don't know your village as well as you thought.'

'So it seems.'

She put out her hand then, clasped his, and then quickly stretched up and kissed him lightly on the cheek. 'Thank you again,' she said. 'Both of you.' Then she was opening the gate, closing it carefully behind her and tiptoeing up the path to the front door.

Hal waited until she had unlocked the door and gone inside. Then, mounting his bicycle, he rode away.

As he pedalled back through the silent village he thought back to several of the things that she had said. She'd given him quite a lot to think about. And nothing that she had said had given him any contentment.

To his surprise he found that Rowan was waiting for him by the gate.

'I thought you'd be in bed by now,' he said as he wheeled his bicycle into the drive.

She closed the gate behind him and stayed there, leaning on it. 'I wanted to wait for you,' she said.

He propped his bicycle against the gatepost and went to stand beside her. He felt unsettled from his conversation with Alison.

'It was a really good evening,' Rowan said.

'Yes, it was.'

'And what a beautiful night now . . .'

As she spoke she looked up at the sky and he felt the brush of her shoulder against his upper arm. He followed her glance upwards to where the Milky Way sprawled in its great curving arc. 'The night has a thousand eyes,' he said, echoing the words she had spoken on the night of their very first meeting. On that night, after leaving the restaurant, they had stood at the gate of her little cottage, and she had looked up at the stars. 'The night has a thousand eyes . . .' she'd said, and he'd asked her, 'What does that line come from? I've often heard it over the years.'

'From a poem – by Bourdillon,' she'd answered. 'I learnt it years ago – after discovering it in some book. I was at a very impressionable age then. I remember I used to recite it – for my own pleasure only, you understand. It was lovely to wallow in such – romanticism.' Then, when he'd asked her to, she'd recited the poem for him.

> The night has a thousand eyes,
> And the day but one;
> Yet the light of the bright world dies
> With the dying sun.
>
> The mind has a thousand eyes,
> And the heart but one;
> Yet the light of a whole life dies
> When love is done.

Earlier that past day he'd hoped for nothing more than to spend the night in her bed. And although he'd still wanted that, very much, there had come the sudden, almost unconscious, realization that there was more to be gained. So much more. So: so much for his half-formed hopes; he'd ended the evening by kissing her on the cheek and shaking her hand. . . .

Funny, he thought now, how easily one's aim could be deflected. And by such a simple thing. It was her reciting of the poem that had done it – that, coming after their time together in the restaurant. The whole course of his life had been changed.

Now, looking back to that night he thought, briefly, of the things that had happened in between: their years in London together, the success of *Spectre*. Adam . . . And now here they were once more in the country; just the two of them again; and, as before, standing by a gate and looking up at the sky. They'd come full circle.

The memory of Adam brought back to him the thought of how much he would love to have another child. Another son. And how much Rowan wanted it too. But would they ever get what they wanted? They'd never once throughout their five years of marriage used any form of birth control. And yet Rowan had conceived only the once. Yet, the doctors had said, there was no reason why she shouldn't again. . . . At the school where he'd taught he'd watched the children of some parents appear year after year, like clones, one after another, with sickening regularity; as one had left for a higher grade so he'd be replaced by a younger one coming up. There was no fairness.

Maybe here, though, in Moorstone, things would be different. If the doctors were right then this place could be the answer. Rowan, with the tension of city life behind her, was growing happier and more relaxed each day. So who could tell? – perhaps in time . . .

'Come on,' he said. Taking hold of his bicycle he put his other arm around her shoulder and briefly hugged her to him. 'Come on, it's time to go in.'

Inside the house they turned off the lights, went upstairs and got undressed. Rowan was first in and out of the bathroom and when Hal emerged from it a few minutes afterwards he found her sitting in her dressing-gown on top of the bed-clothes, supported by the pillows that she had propped against the headboard. As he sat on the edge of the bed she smiled at him, then reached out and switched off the lamp.

'Now I can't see a damn thing,' he said.

'You will – in a minute or two. The moon's so bright.'

He felt her fingers touch the back of his hand, and rest there. Then, gradually, in the pale light that flooded in from the night sky she took shape before him. Squeezing his hand, she said: 'It was a lovely evening, wasn't it?'

'Very nice.'

'And I think Alison enjoyed it too.'

'I'm sure she did.'

'Did you like her?'

'Very much.'

'Not too much, though, I hope.' She smiled as she said this. He grinned back at her.

'What d'you want me to say?'

'Oh – everything – nothing . . .'

He moved closer to her, bent forward and kissed her softly on the mouth. She kissed him back and then moved lower in the bed so that she lay flat, he leaning above her, gazing down. In the dimness she looked about nineteen.

He wore nothing beneath his bathrobe and he lowered his body to hers and pressed his rampant hardness against her.

'I love you, Ro. So much.'

He pulled off his bathrobe, undid the loose cord about her waist and found that she too, under her dressing-gown, was naked. He spread its folds on either side of her, like wings, on the bed. Resting on his knees he straddled her waist. He felt her hand brush his thigh, then touch his rigid flesh and grasp it. Arching his back he pressed forward into the circle of her hand, his own fingers reaching down behind him, finding her moist and ready. For long, ecstatic moments he revelled in the sensations that came from her fingers and the moving of his own, and then, when another second would surely have brought about his climax, he changed his position, knelt beside her and covered her face with kisses.

With all the time in the world he moved his mouth from her forehead to her toes; lips lingering, tongue probing and exploring, while beneath him she moaned her joy, wild hands clutching at his hair, his shoulders. '*Hal . . . Hal . . . Hal . . .*' He would have entered her then, but she breathed, 'Not yet, not yet,' and urged him onto his back beside her. And then the initiative was taken by her, and as her hands, her mouth began their tour he spread wide, wide his legs and arms and gave himself up completely to the almost unbearable pleasure of her touch.

At last she lay beside him again. And then beneath him.

Moving gently – as if he would restrain his passion – he guided his sex slowly into her until he was deep inside. Then, all restraint vanishing, taken by the overpowering sensation, he began to move faster within her – long, rhythmic thrusts – and so deep – as if he would sheath his whole body within her own. On and on, together, their bodies moved – his pounding against her; hers rising up to meet the violence of his thrusts as if she would never get enough of him.

At the very peak, as she gasped and cried beneath him in the climax of her ecstasy he heard the groans torn from his own mouth as, shuddering, he filled her with his seed.

Afterwards they lay beside one another, her head against his sweat-drenched shoulder, their breathing slowing, growing more regular. After a time he eased himself free, raised himself on one elbow and peered down at her. Gently he brushed aside a lock of damp hair that lay plastered to her forehead. She opened her eyes then and gazed up at him. 'My Hal,' she said.

'You bet your life.'

His feeling for her now was all tenderness, added to which was his realization that he had never before known her to be so uninhibited in their love-making. Tonight she had wanted him as much as he had wanted her – and she had demonstrated that wanting, so clearly, taking from his body a pleasure that, in her desire, was both new and totally overwhelming.

How had such a difference come about, he asked himself – knowing the answer all the time. The answer was clear. It was obvious. It was this place; it was Moorstone that had given her her peace and set her free.

For a moment there came to him a memory of the disquieting thoughts and questions that his conversation with Alison had planted in his mind. With a mental, sweeping gesture he pushed it all away from him. So Moorstone wasn't perfect. So what? What place was? The important thing was that it was the place for them – Rowan and him. He looked again into her smiling eyes. Yes – Moorstone might not be ideal – but it would do.

10

When Rowan rang the bell at The Laurels the door was opened by a tall, elegant woman with dark, greying hair. Giving a bright, wide smile she said: 'You must be Mrs Graham. I'll tell Alison you're here.' As she turned to usher Rowan into the hall Alison appeared on the stairs. 'Hello,' she called, 'I'm all ready to go.'

With the front door closed behind them the two set off down the path. Rowan's bicycle was standing outside at the edge of the road. 'Shall I bring it in?' she asked.

'Yes, you'd better. Though I'm quite sure it would be safe there . . .'

Rowan wheeled the machine through and propped it against the grey-stone, ivy-covered wall. 'Did you get all your work done?' she said.

'Yes. I did it all this morning and Miss Carroll says she won't need me again till later this afternoon.' Alison turned and glanced up at the upper windows of the house. 'She's resting at the moment. She's been working very hard this past week – trying to get her book finished. And she's probably been over-doing it a bit. Still, she's in good hands; Miss Allardice is what you'd term an Efficient Body.'

'Is that who answered the door to me? Miss Allardice?'

'Yes, she's the housekeeper.' Alison paused, then said: 'Well, you still want to go for a walk?'

'Oh, yes. I've come dressed for it, and it's such a beautiful day.'

'Fine.' Alison checked that she had her cigarettes with her. 'Where would you like to go?'

Rowan peered away over to the north-west. 'I'd like to go up to the Stone,' she said. 'I see it all the time from our windows and from the village street. I'd like to see it closer too.'

'Okay. We can take the old bridle path, and then go through the wood.'

Together they walked along the road for some hundred yards or so, then turned left and began to make their way along a rough path that led beside a hedgerow. The day was warm. Both women wore blue jeans and sturdy shoes; their steps sounded firm on the surface of the old pathway. In the hedgerow the hawthorn was in full bloom, its fragrant scent touching them as they passed by. Moving beneath a group of tall poplars Rowan saw several peacock butterflies rise high up into the air from the brambles and dance about in a mad up-and-down chase.

Intermittently the girls talked of this and that. Rowan spoke of her work on her children's stories; of its pleasures and its difficulties. Underlying all her words, though, was the satisfaction she felt at the knowledge that she was doing something truly constructive again. 'There was a time,' she said, 'when I thought that was all past – my own attempts at writing . . .' She had never told Alison anything about Adam. 'But now my interest in it is all back again. And I'm sure it's all due to this place. And once I'm feeling a hundred per cent again I know I shall really be able to make some progress.'

'Why, what's wrong?' Alison asked. 'Aren't you well?'

Rowan shrugged. 'I don't know what it is. I just haven't been feeling terribly bright these past few days. I have this kind of – lassitude, and not much appetite. And I keep getting this rather – queasy feeling. It's probably nothing worth bothering about. It's just a little debilitating, that's all. Makes work a bit of an effort. I had thought it might be because my period's a bit late. It was due the day before yesterday.'

'Does it sometimes affect you in that way?'

'No. Well, it never has done in the past. But there, I'm never ever late. It comes bang on time every month, lasts a bare three days and is gone. You could set your watch by me. – But anyway, I know it's nothing to do with that.'

'What makes you so sure?'

Rowan grinned. 'Because this morning I discovered that Hal's suffering with the same symptoms.'

Alison laughed. 'Well, yes, I think you might have a point

there.' Then she went on, 'But perhaps you ought to go and see Paul Cassen. He's marvellous. Not like those bloody city doctors who haven't even got time to remember who you are. He's really caring and thorough.'

'Oh, it's probably just due to the change of diet. Or we've picked up some kind of flu bug or something. . . .'

'Maybe. It sounds like something I had three or four weeks back. Paul Cassen fixed me up in no time at all.'

Over to the left of the path was a wide wood and they cut into its north-east corner, where in its shade the wood sorrel bloomed and the wood anemones were spread in a white carpet. Emerging into the sunlight once more they moved downhill across open ground towards a line of tall chestnut trees beyond which the ground rose sharply again. Some-where a cuckoo called. Since they'd started out they hadn't seen another human being. They might have been miles from the nearest human habitation; there was just space, blue sky and green fields and trees. Rowan's sense of freedom was very real.

Passing beneath the wide arms of the chestnut trees they started up the grassy slope of the hill. As they climbed, Rowan saw, rising up beyond its summit, the peak of a second hill, topped not with grass and brambles like this one, but with a huge crest of stone that reared up, dark against the May sky, its northern edge jutting like a pouting lip far out over the side of the hill on which it stood.

'Well, there you are,' said Alison, 'that's the Stone.'

'It's so dramatic,' Rowan said. 'Right out here amid all this green – springing up out of the hilltop. Is it some kind of geo-logical freak?'

'I don't think so.' Alison shook her head doubtfully. 'I think it must have been brought here in ancient times. Like with Stonehenge and those other stones. Probably for use in some pagan rites or something.'

They moved on upward, over the top of the hill, down the other side and up again towards the Stone. Drawing closer to it, Rowan saw that its face in line with the gradually sloping hillside had been hewn to form crude steps, shallow and very wide. She followed as Alison started up them. At the top she found that within its roughly hewn rim the surface had been cut quite flat – which had been impossible to discern from below. The platform covered a wide area – about twenty yards wide by thirty or forty long, she reckoned. She walked along it towards the lip that jutted out over the almost sheer side of the hill. Behind her Alison's voice came: 'Aren't you afraid of heights? There're no mattresses or trampolines down there. Just a bunch of rocks. And they're a *long* way down.'

Smiling over her shoulder, Rowan saw that Alison was standing at the top of the steps. 'I am afraid of heights,' she said. 'I'm terrified. But don't worry – I shan't go near the edge.'

She didn't. She came to a halt some five or six yards from the point where the rock platform just stopped, the lip suspended in space, high above the scattered rocks below.

When she turned again she saw that Alison had seated herself on the top step and was lighting a cigarette. 'It's amazing,' Rowan said, 'you can see for miles from up here.' She looked over to her right, to the east where the village nestled in the hollow of the hills. 'I can see our house there – so clearly.' She raised her hands to her eyes, curling her fingers into binoculars. 'Oh, yes, and there's Hal there – pretending to work.'

'Only pretending?'

'I'm afraid so.'

Rowan had touched on a subject she had no wish to pursue. She turned her back on the view of the village, moved across the surface of the stone and sat down beside Alison on the step. Alison said:

'Have you heard how your Mrs Prescot's sister's getting on? Is she any better?'

'About the same. Mrs Prescot phoned a couple of days ago. Poor thing. It's so worrying for her.'

Alison nodded. 'I'm sure.' After a pause she asked: 'And how's it working out with Mrs Palfrey? Is she still working like a Trojan?'

'Oh, she's incredible. Paul Cassen was right when he said she was very able. She is. I'm well satisfied.'

'And Hal?'

'Well – she's been with us less than a week – and he says it's much too soon to form any judgement. And he's right, of course. Though he's not too enamoured, you can tell.'

'Does he say why?'

'I don't think he even knows. But for some reason he just doesn't care for her very much. He didn't want to hire her in the first place.'

The talk moved on to other things. As she lit her third cigarette Alison said, 'We'd better go when I've finished this.'

'Will there be more work waiting for you?'

'A bit, I expect. Nothing worth hurrying back for; nothing that wouldn't keep till tomorrow. I really don't understand why Miss Carroll went to all the trouble of hiring somebody from outside. I'm sure there are plenty of local girls who could easily do what I'm doing there.' She shrugged. 'Still, it's her money.' A little silence fell, then she added: 'Anyway, I'm leaving in a few weeks.'

Rowan looked at her in surprise and dismay. 'I thought you were going to be here for a year . . .'

'Well, yes, I was – originally. But near the end of May Geoff's coming back to do some business connected with his job – and I've decided to return with him when he goes back out east. He's got a nice flat there now, he says – and it's a good opportunity for me to see a little more of the world. The main thing is, though, I shall be with him. That's what really matters. I do so hate it – our being apart.'

Rowan's feeling of disappointment made it difficult for her to smile. 'Well, I'm glad for you,' she said. 'But I'm really sorry – from my point of view – that you're going.'

'Yes, that part of it's a shame.' Alison nodded. 'Now that we've just met and find that we get on well together. But there –' She grinned, as if hugging her knowledge to her. 'I can hardly believe it: I shall be seeing Geoff soon.'

'I'm looking forward to meeting him. He sounds pretty special.'

'He is, believe me. He's the best thing that ever happened to me.'

After a moment or two Rowan asked: 'How long have you known – that you'll be leaving?'

'Two days. I got a letter from Geoff. I couldn't tell you earlier because I hadn't told Miss Carroll.'

'And she knows now?'

'Yes. Oh, I felt awful about that – telling her. I told her this morning. She was a bit taken aback, as you can imagine. But I think she understands. She was very nice about it.'

'So now she'll have to find somebody else . . .'

'I suppose so.' She sighed. 'Ah, well, it can't be helped.' She stubbed out her cigarette and got to her feet. 'We'd better get back.' Looking around her she added with a wry smile, 'And I'll be bloody glad to get off this heap of rock. For some reason it gives me the creeps.'

II

From his desk Hal had watched Rowan ride away to keep her appointment with Alison.

His head was aching and there was a slight but constant unsettled feeling at the pit of his stomach. It made the effort of work more difficult than ever. All morning he had stayed in his study, either sitting hunched over his loose-leaf writing pad or just staring into space. His pencils, sharpened and unused, stood before him in their pot like a battalion of soldiers. He'd got nowhere at all.

It wasn't long after Rowan had gone that Tim Farson, his agent, telephoned. How were things going? Farson asked. How was the new book progressing?

The publication of *Spectre at the Feast* last year was to be followed this coming autumn by Hal's sixth novel, *Kill or Cure* – his work on which he had long since finished. His concern

now was with a new one – as yet untitled – which was intended
for publication next year. If he ever got it done, that was. At the
rate he was going it was something he couldn't be sure of.

Now, lying in answer to Farson's questions he said that
the book was going well, adding that it should be completed
within another three or four months.

'Fine,' Farson said. 'I just wondered. And wondered how
you are, too. It's been a while since we had a chance to talk . . .'

'You're right,' Hal agreed, 'it has.'

'Do you get up to town at all these days? Or are you too
busy?'

'I plan on coming up very soon,' Hal said. He hadn't made
any such plan, but the sudden thought was an attractive one.
'Early next week,' he added. 'I shall probably stay for a couple
of days.'

'Well, maybe we could have lunch.'

'Good idea. Which day would suit you?'

'You say . . . Monday or Tuesday . . . ?'

'Tuesday would be fine.'

'Can you come to the office about twelve-thirty?'

'I'll see you then.'

As Hal replaced the receiver he was aware of how eagerly
he'd jumped at the excuse to get back to the city – if only for a
short while – and how he was now looking forward to it.

Pleasant as the prospect was, though, it in no way helped
him with his most immediate problem: the book.

The idea for the new novel had been conceived some weeks
before the move from London, and in the excitement of its
discovery he had worked quickly and enthusiastically to get a
roughly-constructed plot down on paper. That done, he had
begun his first draft, working long and earnestly, and confi-
dent, as in the past, that the book's development would follow
its usual course.

And it had gone well. And then the move from London
had loomed on the horizon. With that threatening he had
worked even harder, trying to get as much as possible behind
him while he had the chance. There hadn't been much time,

though. So much in the way of preparation had had to be done in connection with the move, and very quickly all thoughts of any serious work had had to be put aside. And so it would be, he had told himself, until the moving business was over and some kind of order in their lives was again discernible.

Well, they had been in Moorstone for a month now and the moving in was over. By this time, with their lives fairly ordered again he should be deeply involved in the book once more; he had the time and the opportunity . . .

But it hadn't happened as he'd expected, as he'd hoped. What was it that had got in the way? At this stage in his work – halfway through the first draft – he was usually so passionately obsessed with what he was doing that the hours flew by and he'd often find himself resenting any interruptions that might occur. Not now. Right now he would have welcomed any interruptions at all.

Perhaps, he said to himself, he'd feel more like work when this debilitating feeling of sickness had left him. As it was he had no energy at all. And no appetite either. At lunch he hadn't felt like eating at all. Like Rowan, though, he'd forced himself to do so. Neither had wanted to offend Mrs Palfrey . . . At the back of his mind, however, was the vague thought that his lack of drive and enthusiasm was unconnected with his slight, temporary illness. Whatever it was, though, he could only trust that it would soon pass. It *must*. Not only did he have to get going on the book but soon he would have to begin work on the screenplay for *Spectre at the Feast*.

After sitting unmoving at his desk for a few minutes longer he got up, went outside and took his bicycle from the garage. Seconds later he was pedalling away.

Heading nowhere in particular he moved in a westerly direction with the village on his left. Up ahead of him in the distance he could see the dark shape of the Stone rising up. He must go there one day, he said to himself – get a closer view of it. Not today, though.

About twenty minutes after setting out he had half circled

the village. Now he re-entered it, rode into the High Street and parked his bicycle at the kerb.

He was idly wandering from shop front to shop front when he saw the painting.

It hung in the window of an antique shop, over to the right and partly obscured by an old hanging brass lamp. The framed canvas, quite small, depicted a line of trees against the sky. Silver birches. He recognized the scene at once, and immediately he could see in his mind the old lady standing forlornly at the edge of the chalkpit, turning, pointing: '*I painted those too – in different lights, different moods . . .*'

But Paul Cassen had told him that never, to his knowledge, had she done any such thing; she'd never painted, he'd said.

Although Hal craned his neck he could see no signature on the picture. The lower left corner of the canvas bore no sign of one, while the lower right was hidden by the lamp. After standing there looking at the picture for some minutes more he went into the shop and approached a young man who sat at a desk writing in a ledger. In answer to Hal's query he said that the painting was the work of a young woman from the village, Mary Hughes. Was he interested in buying the picture? he asked Hal. No, Hal replied, he was merely curious.

Outside on the pavement again he stood and looked once more at the painting. This was no Sunday painter's daubings. This was the work of someone with experience and training; the technique alone gave evidence of that. The colours and the tones were cool and clear, while the paint had been applied in bold, vigorous strokes, giving the impression of sureness and youthful energy.

The subject, though . . . surely those were the trees he had seen before . . .

He stood at the window for some seconds longer, then, with the image of the birches fixed clearly in his mind, got back onto his bicycle and rode away from the village.

Ten minutes later he was deep in the heart of the moorland countryside, pulling to a stop at the side of the road. Yes, he remembered this spot only too well. There was the gap in the hedge. He laid his bicycle down on the narrow grass verge and stepped through the gap into the field beyond.

Reaching the rise in the ground he saw before him once more the chalkpit. The scenes from the past nightmare were vivid in his mind. He thrust them aside and, turning about, sought the line of trees the woman had indicated. And there they were – five slender silver birches – exactly as they'd been captured in the painting he'd just seen.

He looked back to the pit, just briefly, then moved away from it back over the grass towards the hedge. Depression had settled over him like a cloak. He should have stayed at home. . . .

He took a roundabout way back to Crispin's House, all the time skirting the edge of the village. So much of the route was unfamiliar to him. Then, just before he turned right onto the familiar Rookery Road he saw on his left a sign saying *Primrose House*. Beyond it was a tall old building set back amongst green lawns and almost hidden by surrounding trees. He came to a halt and, astride his bicycle, stood peering through the foliage.

So this was Primrose House. And, according to Alison, a mental home . . .

Surely, though, she must be mistaken. Moorstone was so small. How could it possibly warrant the necessity of such an institution . . . ?

With a final glance at the building he got back on his bicycle and headed for home.

There was music coming from Crispin's House.

At first he thought Rowan must be back and was playing the radio or a record. Her bicycle was not in the garage, though. After leaving his own bicycle there he moved closer to the partly open sitting room window and realized that the sound was actually coming from the piano within. Furthermore, the instrument was being played by someone who knew what it was all about. And that definitely excluded Rowan. She, in her piano studies, had never gone beyond the fourth year.

He recognized the music. It was something by Chopin,

familiar to him from his own early years. At the moment the
playing of it was reaching the end of the first section. At times
the music came to his ears a little haltingly – sometimes the
rippling notes stumbling, like a tired runner losing his rhythm.
Nonetheless, it sounded to him quite brilliant.

The middle episode began, its beautiful melody less
demanding of dexterity. Here in this much slower passage the
notes were struck more surely, and with great feeling and tenderness. He listened, rapt, as the slow, lyrical section ended and
the fingers took off again, attempting the rippling cadences of
the fast, difficult closing passage. And here the music seemed
beyond the fingers' ability. After stumbling a couple of times
the notes, in mid-passage, came to an abrupt end.

Entering the sitting room a few moments later he found
Mrs Palfrey sitting at the piano looking down at the keyboard.
She had her back to him but then at the sound of his step she
turned, saw him and got quickly to her feet. She looked flus-
tered and a little embarrassed.

'I'm sorry, Mr Graham,' she said, 'I didn't hear you come
in. I wouldn't have – I mean . . .' Her words trailed off and she
briefly lowered her eyes.

'Please – don't apologize.' He smiled, trying to put her at
her ease. 'I was listening to you, outside. I couldn't help it.' He
paused. 'That piece – it's Chopin, isn't it?'

'Yes. His "Fantaisie-Impromptu in C Sharp Minor." It's a
very popular work.'

He nodded. 'It's lovely. And – well, I never would have
dreamed that you could play so well.'

At this she gave a little smile. 'Oh, I don't play well, Mr
Graham. Not now. Though once I did.'

'You obviously studied for a very long time.'

'Oh, yes, years ago. Yes . . . I had the very best teachers.'
Raising her head slightly she added with a note of pride: 'Oh,
yes, I could play. I've played before great people. Heads of
state, kings and queens. In my time I've played for them all.'
She smiled again and gave a little shake of her head. 'Ah, but
what's the point in reliving the past. It's all over.' She looked

down at her misshapen hands. 'I wouldn't get far with these now, would I? I'm surprised I managed to do as well as I did with that little piece. . . .' She lowered the lid of the piano over the keys. Turning back to face him she asked: 'Did you ever study any musical instrument?'

'No, I'm afraid not. Though I often wish I had. Rowan plays, though – ' he grinned as he gestured towards the piano, ' – a little.'

She gave a solemn little nod. 'Ah, yes. That's – interesting.' Her tone changed then, becoming a little brisker. 'Would you like me to make you some tea? You generally have some about this time – and as Mrs Graham is out – '

'No, I don't think so, thank you.' He felt awkward in her presence. He always did. And now, after what she had told him about her past musical career he felt even more at a disadvantage. 'I think I'll just get myself a glass of water – and take an aspirin,' he said. 'Then maybe take a bath.'

'Have you got a headache?'

'Yes. I've been feeling a bit sick too.' He smiled. The awkwardness was still there. 'Not to worry. It'll pass.'

The water was soft and soothing and he lay back, trying to relax in the comfort. It wasn't easy, though. His head was pounding and his brain besieged. His visit to the chalkpit had brought back so vividly his memories of Miss Larkin. He kept seeing her running down the slope to the brink of the pit; leaping up and out . . . the sight of her again as he had found her at the bottom. He pictured again the line of silver birches nearby – and the painting of them in the shop window. His view of the secluded house off Rookery Road . . . Primrose House . . . that came into his mind too.

And then Mrs Palfrey . . . He saw her sitting at the piano, her stiff fingers refusing to do as they were bidden. That picture was disturbing as well. Had she been a concert pianist? How, then, could she have come to this? – In her later years to be cooking and cleaning in the house of strangers . . . ?

He was suddenly aware of the ringing of the extension telephone in the bedroom next door. Mrs Palfrey would answer it downstairs. No matter, anyway; he wasn't moving.

The ringing stopped and the house was silent again. Only for a minute, though. The next thing he heard was a sharp tap on the bathroom door and then Mrs Palfrey's rather agitated voice.

' – Mr Graham – ?'

'Yes, what is it?' he called. He was aware of the irritableness in his tone.

Her answer came hurriedly, breathlessly:

'Someone's just phoned to say that – that Mrs Graham's had a terrible accident!'

Water streaming from him, Hal was out of the bath and getting into his bathrobe. Heart thudding he opened the door and looked into Mrs Palfrey's pale face. 'For God's sake, what's happened?' he cried out. 'Is she all right?'

'I don't know. I don't know. It was some woman from the village. It happened in the High Street, she said. They've taken Mrs Graham to Mr Lockyer's house.'

'Oh, dear God.' Hal shook his head distractedly, blind panic mounting with every passing moment. 'All right,' he said at last, 'you go on downstairs and wait by the phone. I'll be there in a second.'

Barely two minutes later he had dressed and, still damp under his clothes, was hurrying into the sitting room where Mrs Palfrey was pacing the carpet. Even as he moved towards the telephone it rang. He picked it up. 'Yes?'

'Mr Graham?'

'Yes.'

'Hello, my name is Lockyer. I don't want to – '

' – My wife,' Hal interrupted, ' – is she all right?'

'Yes – that's what I'm calling to tell you.'

'You're sure she's all right.'

'Yes, really. Don't worry about her . . .'

'Thank God . . .' Hal breathed a deep sigh of relief. In his palm the receiver was damp with sweat. 'Someone phoned just now and said enough to – well, to scare the life out of me . . .' Then he said again, 'You're quite sure she's okay.'

'Yes, really. She came off her bicycle and had a nasty fall – so of course she's very shaken. She's hurt her wrist, too, I'm afraid. But apart from that she's all right.'

'What has she *done* to her wrist?'

'I don't know. She might have broken it – or it might just be a bad sprain. Anyway, I've phoned Dr Cassen and he said to bring her round to see him at once.'

'Is she still with you now?'

'Yes. She asked me to call you.'

Quickly, Hal took down Lockyer's address. 'I'll be there right away,' he said. 'I'll leave at once.'

As he put down the phone he turned and saw Mrs Palfrey. He'd forgotten she was there. Her still pale face was sharply etched with lines of distress. 'It's all right,' he said to her. 'She's okay.'

'I heard you say something about her wrist . . . She's hurt her wrist, you said . . .'

'Yes, but we don't know how badly. We'll soon find out.'

He left her standing there, got the keys to the car and hurried outside.

12

The accident had been caused by two young boys whose ball had rolled into the roadway, right beneath the wheels of Rowan's bicycle. Violently she had swerved to avoid it – at the same time too swiftly applying the brakes. The next moment she had lain sprawled on the tarmac.

Apart from the two boys – who stood staring and open-mouthed – David Lockyer had been the first on the scene and after establishing that Rowan didn't seem to be seriously hurt had taken her into his house opposite The Swan. There she had sat in an armchair, shaking and pale-faced, her right wrist painfully swelling.

In her trembling left hand she had held the glass of brandy that Lockyer had poured, taken a sip and then burst into tears. He had taken the glass away from her then, handed her a Kleenex and stood quietly by while she'd dabbed at her eyes.

'I'm okay,' she'd murmured after a while. 'It's just the shock, mostly, that's all. I'll be fine in a minute.'

Her swollen wrist, though, was not fine, and after looking at it Lockyer had said they'd better get it examined. Shortly after that he had phoned Paul Cassen.

As he'd dialled Cassen's number and spoken into the receiver Rowan had become aware that at no time had he asked her who she was. He hadn't needed to; there he was on the phone speaking her name. He had known her identity just as she had known his. Part of the business of living in Moorstone. . . .

He'd gone out to the kitchen then, and she'd sat in silence in the quiet room and looked around her. The furniture was old and from different periods. The colours were softly muted. A few books lay on the sofa, more on the cluttered coffee table. On the lid of the grand piano sheets of music manuscript paper lay scattered or in untidy piles, whilst in the midst stood a bust of Beethoven, a violin case and a vase of wilting roses. The whole room had that slight look of carelessness that she associated with the idea of preoccupied, once married men now living alone.

As she turned her attention to the pictures on the walls – watercolour landscapes along with a few photographs of musicians – she realized that there was nothing at all in the room to remind anyone of the man's past career – a career that, through numerous successful stage, television and film appearances, had made his face known throughout the country.

When he came back into the room he was carrying a tray. He set it down and began to pour tea. As he handed her a cup he said, 'When you're feeling a bit better we'll get you over to see Paul Cassen; let him take a look at that wrist.'

She regarded him as he spoke. She was beginning to feel

a little calmer. Watching him, remembering his face from the television screen it was as if, now, she were seeing him with new eyes. Although he had the same blunt features and slightly rusty-brown hair, the look of him was somehow different. Now he was real. He seemed taller, too, in the flesh, and better looking. Younger, as well; he couldn't be much more than thirty. There was something else, too, she realized – and it had to do with the reality of the moment. This was not the famous David Lockyer playing a role; this was *he*; the concern in his face and voice were not assumed.

'. . . something else we should do,' he said as she sipped her tea. 'We'd better phone your husband and let him know that you're all right. Word travels fast in this place and you wouldn't want him to get some garbled, inaccurate account from someone who doesn't know the facts.' He paused. 'Shall I give him a call?'

'Please . . .' She gave him the number.

He moved to the phone. 'Would you like to talk to him . . . ?'

'No . . .' She knew that if she spoke to Hal she'd start to cry. 'Just tell him I'm all right. Ask him to come and get me.'

She listened then to his side of the conversation with Hal. When it was over Lockyer said: 'Well, I was right; and I was too late. Some busybody had got to him first. He was obviously fearing the worst. Still, it'll be all right now.' He smiled at her. 'He'll be round soon.'

They talked as they waited for Hal, and Rowan asked Lockyer whether he ever missed his acting career.

'Never,' he told her. 'I never even think about it now. It's all part of the past. I'm much happier now, writing my music.' He shrugged. 'I don't make as much money, of course, but that's not always the important thing. I'm doing now what I really want to do.'

'I thought you were doing that before – going by what I read at different times . . .'

He smiled. 'You mustn't always believe what you read.'

'No, I suppose not. How did you come to settle here in Moorstone?'

In answer he told her that after learning about the village from one of its inhabitants he had come to see it for himself – with the idea of staying for a few weeks while he studied the script of a new play in which he planned to appear. He was looking for peace and quiet, he said – which were not always available in his often too-hectic London life.

'I found both here,' he said with a smile, 'and some real friends into the bargain. Not like in the theatre world. There – well, one's so-called friends are all so – here today and gone tomorrow. There's no stability at all. Not as there is in a place like this. Anyway, among the friends I made here were an old fellow and his sister. Leclerc, their name was. They're both dead now. But they were marvellous to me. When I got ill they looked after me. The sister had been a nurse. They even took me into their house so that they could care for me properly. And – ' he spread his hands, ' – that's how it happened. When I recovered I decided to stay. I never did do that play. When eventually I went back to London it was just for the briefest of visits – just to settle up my affairs there.'

'The same kind of thing happened to Paul Cassen,' Rowan said. 'Coming here, liking it and deciding to stay. *And* finding a new career – '

As she finished speaking there came a ring at the doorbell.

'That must be Hal,' she said.

With the effects of the shock still lurking just beneath the surface she had burst into tears when Hal had wrapped his arms around her in Lockyer's untidy sitting room. Now, though, she was calm again and while she got into the car Hal took her bicycle from where it had been left in Lockyer's small, neat garden and loaded it into the back. Then, after thanking Lockyer for all his help he got in beside her and they set off for the doctor's house. It was Sandra who let them in. After directing Hal to a comfortable sofa she showed Rowan into Cassen's consulting room. There, Rowan sat before the young doctor and told him what had happened. He examined her wrist and after a little painful probing and manipulating told her that she had sprained it. He bound it with a crepe bandage. 'I'm afraid,' he said, 'you're not going to be able to use this for a while.'

After he had dealt with the minor cuts and grazes on her legs and elbow he asked, 'How are you feeling apart from all this? – generally, I mean . . . ?'

'Oh, okay, I suppose . . .'

'You just suppose?' He laid the back of his hand to her forehead, frowned slightly then put a thermometer into her mouth. Sitting facing her he then took her left hand in his and felt for her pulse. He took the thermometer from her mouth, looked at it and said, 'You have a temperature, you know. Have you been feeling all right?'

She told him then of her lassitude over the past few days, the nauseated feelings that sometimes affected her. 'Though it's not just me,' she added, ' – it's Hal as well.'

'You've both been feeling ill, yet neither one of you has done anything about it? Have you taken anything for it?'

'We got some pills from the chemist – not that they did any good.'

He shook his head, ' – patent medicines,' then went to the door and called out to Hal who came in and sat next to Rowan. After questioning them both at length about their symptoms Cassen wrote out a prescription. 'It sounds as though you've picked up some virus,' he said. 'Here – ' he handed the slip of paper to Hal, ' – this is for both of you. For some medicine. Take it as prescribed. We'll see if that does the trick.'

Hal thanked him and started to get up from the chair. Cassen motioned to him to sit down again. 'When did you last have any kind of physical checkup?' he asked him.

'Oh . . .' Hal shrugged and shook his head. 'God knows. Years ago . . .'

'And you?' Cassen turned to Rowan.

' – Not for a good while . . .'

'Then I think it would be a good idea if you both had one.' He turned back to his desk and opened his diary. 'Let's see now. How about next Monday? Could you both come along then?'

Rowan nodded but Hal said: 'I'm going up to London on Monday.'

'At what time?'

'Oh – late morning, I would think . . .'

'Okay, well come along before you leave. How about nine-thirty? Would that give you enough time?'

'Yes, I suppose so.'

'Fine. Then I'll see you both on Monday morning at nine-thirty.' Cassen stood up. 'And now, Hal, you take Rowan home and see that she gets some rest. That's very important. And both of you take that medicine I've prescribed. Do that and the pair of you will soon be all right again.'

Rowan was lying in bed when the door opened. She saw Hal's head appear and then heard him call her name in a whisper.

'It's okay,' she said, 'I'm awake.' Reaching out with her good hand she switched on the bedside lamp. He came towards her and sat on the edge of the bed. 'You should be asleep,' he said.

'I know. I couldn't, though.'

'Are you all right?'

'Oh, yes. Just a little – melancholy, that's all. But that's only the reaction, I'm sure . . .'

'Poor baby.' He reached out to where her bound wrist lay on the covers. Softly he touched her arm above the bandage. 'How is it?'

'It's a little painful – but okay.'

'And how do you feel generally?'

'About the same.'

'Did you take any of Cassen's medicine?' He indicated the bottle that stood on the bedside table.

'Yes. Did you?'

'Yes. It's foul stuff.'

'It must be good, then.' She paused. 'You said you're going up to London on Monday. When did you arrange that?'

'This afternoon, just after you left. Tim Farson called. We're going to have lunch on Tuesday. But I want to do a few things in the way of research while I'm there. I thought I'd come back on Wednesday. I'll stay at the club.'

'Is that your real reason for going – to see your agent and do research?'

'Yes – why?'

She hesitated before answering. 'You're not *really* happy here, are you, Hal?'

'Well – yes. What makes you say that?'

She shrugged. 'I've watched you sometimes – over the past few days. Sometimes you look like a fish out of water.'

He smiled, rather tentatively. 'Oh, well, I'm just – finding my feet still, that's all. It takes longer for some people to settle, I suppose.'

In the soft glow of the lamp she studied the lines of his face, searching for something that was not in his words. This place was so good for her; she knew it. She'd felt so much better since they'd got here. She desperately wanted Hal to feel equally happy. . . .

'Why don't you come with me to London,' he said. 'We could go to the theatre or the opera or something. It would make a break for you.'

She smiled. 'I don't need a break. No, you go. Do what you have to do.'

'You won't mind being here on your own?'

'Not in the least.' She turned and glanced briefly at the clock. Just after ten-thirty. 'Are you coming to bed soon?' she asked.

'In a while. There's a programme on television I want to watch first.' He got off the bed and stood looking down at her. 'Oh, boy,' he said with a little shake of his head, 'I got a hell of a shock this afternoon . . .' He spoke again of the telephone call that had come while he was in the bath. Rowan gave a wry nod. 'That's what David Lockyer was afraid might happen,' she said. Then she added, 'He was so kind to me.'

'Yes – and I'm very grateful.' Hal smiled. 'It was so interesting for me to meet him, too – after having seen him on the box . . .' He paused. 'How on earth did he come to give it all up and come to live here?'

'I asked him that.' She related Lockyer's story. Afterwards
Hal said:

'Well, if music's his thing now he should have a lot in
common with Mrs Palfrey.'

'What do you mean?'

He told her of how he had returned to the house to find
Mrs Palfrey playing the piano. 'Apparently,' he said, 'she was
once a concert pianist.' As Rowan shook her head in wonderment he added, 'Yes, the people here are full of surprises,
aren't they? Not least Mrs Palfrey.'

'And she certainly surprised *me* today,' Rowan said, 'waiting here, long after she should have gone home – just to see
how I was. My God, she seemed so upset. You'd have thought
I'd been crippled for life or something. And all the questions
– how exactly had I hurt myself? – was I in pain? – what did
the doctor say? She was like some little old mother hen.' She
smiled. 'It was so sweet of her to be so concerned. It was really
quite touching.'

'Yes.'

Hal left then to go back downstairs, returning some time
later and climbing into bed beside her. In the comfort of his
nearness and his warmth she slept.

In the early hours when discomfort in her wrist briefly took
her from her sleep she opened her eyes and saw that the bedside light was on. She glanced at the clock and saw that it was
after two. Next to her Hal was sitting up, propped against his
pillows and smoking a cigarette. Seeing her awaken beside
him he patted her shoulder and brushed his hand against
her hair. 'Hey, go on back to sleep.' Drowsily she nodded and
closed her eyes. As she nestled close to him again there came
into her mind the realization that her period still hadn't come
on. For a few moments she held on to the thought; and then
she was asleep again.

13

The next morning Rowan said she was feeling much better, and by the morning of the following day, Sunday, her wrist – so long as she didn't try to use it – was giving her no pain. In addition, she told Hal, her feelings of nausea and lassitude had practically gone. He looked at her in surprise and realization. 'Mine too,' he said. He had forgotten all about his own illness. Paul Cassen's medicine must be doing the trick. . . .

Hal was so glad they had the house to themselves. After breakfast they sat around reading the papers, drinking coffee, playing records and chatting. Later, when Alison phoned, they asked her round for dinner. They'd expect her, Rowan said, about six-thirty. Hal would be cooking a casserole.

When six o'clock came accompanied by heavy rain Hal phoned Alison and said he'd drive round and pick her up in the car. A few minutes later, after checking on the progress of the food, he took off Rowan's apron and left the house.

His ring at the doorbell of The Laurels was answered by Miss Allardice, who showed him into the drawing room. 'I'll tell Alison you're here,' she said. 'I think she's almost ready.'

Left alone, he looked about him at the wide, spacious room. It spoke of elegance and grace and a great love of beauty. The walls were hung with many paintings, oils and watercolours – from all different periods, from the Renaissance to the present day. He found himself gazing in awe at an original Turner, a Murillo, a Gainsborough. It was like being in an art gallery.

Casting his eyes further along they came to rest on a small modern oil painting: a still-life depicting a loaf of bread with onions on a blue dish. He recognized the style at once. That bold application of colour, the incisive, sure brushwork. Next to it was a landscape, a view of the Stone. They were both by Mary Hughes, the artist whose work he'd seen in the shop window.

At the sound of an opening door he turned and saw an old woman coming towards him. Her old-fashioned skirts fell almost to her shoes, while about her shoulders hung a crocheted shawl embroidered with flowers of silk and little beads of jet. Her grey hair was dressed in a single plait that was wound in a thick coil about the crown of her head. She looked like someone from another time.

Smiling warmly at him she held out one small, beringed hand to be shaken. As Hal took it she said, her voice light and rather musical:

'Mr Graham, Miss Allardice told me you were here. I've been wanting to meet you. I'm Edith Carroll . . .'

In reply Hal said that he'd been looking forward to meeting her, adding, however, his regret that he had not as yet had time to read any of her books.

She waved his apologies aside, telling him that the same went for herself. 'I know only too well what it's like when one's involved in one's own writing,' she said. 'Time becomes so precious; there's little of it left over for anything else.' She gestured for him to sit down on the sofa and then sat facing him from a small velvet-covered armchair. They talked for two or three minutes on individual methods of working, following which she turned and glanced at the wall near which he had been standing. 'But I think that's what I'd really like to have done, though,' she said, ' – be a painter. I do so admire such talent. Unfortunately, however, I've never had the slightest ability at all in that direction.' She smiled at him. 'Do you like my collection?'

'Oh – so much. It's rather – overwhelming.'

She gave a nod of satisfaction. 'It is, isn't it? I agree.' She got up and moved across the room, coming to a halt in front of a small Pasmore nude. 'I love them so much. I couldn't be without them now.'

Rising from the sofa, Hal went to her side. She turned to him as he approached.

'It's taken me years to collect them all. Years.' Her bright eyes swept the wall, touching the pictures one by one. Standing beside her, Hal shook his head in admiration, at a loss for the right words. 'They're just – magnificent,' he said.

She turned her smile to him. 'It makes me happy to see your appreciation. But there, Alison tells me that you have a collection of your own.'

'Oh, hardly a collection. I've got three. An Andrew Wyeth, a Picasso etching and a drawing by Hockney.' He added, 'And I love them very much.'

He moved with her then as she stepped from one picture to another. On each one she spoke a few words, briefly and to the point. When they came to the still-life and the Moorstone landscape Hal said:

'This painter – she's one of the villagers, so I'm told.'

'Mary Hughes, yes. She is now. Though I knew of her work before she came to live here. She was a student at the Royal College – one of their brighter lights. Oh, that was a thrill for me when I learned that she had come to work in Moorstone.' She indicated the still-life and the landscape. 'She did these soon after she arrived here. I consider myself very lucky to have got them.' She turned towards a window. The rain had stopped now, and through the sunlit trees Hal could see the winding road and the thatched roof of a large, white-walled cottage. 'She lives there,' Miss Carroll said.

A sound from behind them brought Hal's head around and he saw Alison enter the room. She hoped she hadn't kept him waiting too long, she said, to which he replied, not at all; it had given him the chance to meet Miss Carroll.

Now the old lady gave him her hand once more and said that he must come back and see her and her pictures again sometime. 'But wait three or four weeks,' she told him, ' – then my book should be finished and I shall have time to relax.' She looked from him to Alison. 'You two are young and have the knowledge that there's plenty of time before you. When one gets old, though, it's a different story. The time goes so fast and one is grateful for every year . . .' Then she brushed away her words with a little movement of her hand. 'But enough. It's not a problem for you; it's only a problem for me. And who is

interested in such depressing thoughts – especially now that
the sun is out again?' She smiled warmly. 'It's going to be a
beautiful evening, so you two go off and enjoy yourselves
while you can.'

Outside, Hal and Alison got into the car. Hal fished for his
cigarettes, gave one to Alison and then lit them. Alison said:
'She's quite something, isn't she?'

'Yes, she is.'

'She's absolutely obsessed with her work, you know. And
with getting this current book finished.'

'I gathered that; the way she kept on about time. Still, I
suppose it's understandable, at her age. What's the book like
– the one she's writing? Having been typing it you must have a
pretty good idea . . .'

'Oh, I like it, very much. But what I find particularly impres-
sive is her knowledge of the past. Her feeling for it. All the
detail and the colour – it's all there.'

Hal started the car and they set off back along the road.
Slowing for the turning at the crossroads he saw before him
the thatched, white-walled cottage that Miss Carroll had
pointed out. Quickly checking in the mirror to see that nothing was coming up behind he changed direction and instead of
turning right continued straight on.

The house was a little way down on the left-hand side.
He drove past it fairly slowly; curious. Glancing over into the
garden he caught a brief glimpse of a bending female figure.
Twenty yards further on he came to a stop and switched off
the engine. 'What's the matter?' Alison asked.

'Just hang on here, will you? I'll be back in a minute.' He
got out of the car, turned and walked back along the road to
the gate of the cottage. Looking over the gate he saw a young,
slim woman standing on the path trying to unroll a piece of
chicken wire. She wore old jeans and sweater and wellingtons.
Her hair was long and dark, hanging loosely about her shoulders. He realized he'd seen her in the village on two or three
occasions.

'Excuse me,' he said, 'are you Miss Hughes . . . ?'

'Yes . . .' Her smile was tentative as she turned to him.

'Hello,' he said. ' – My name's Hal Graham. I've recently come to live in the village. . . .'

'Ah.' She nodded and her smile grew wider. Then she raised the roll of wire and gestured briefly towards a shrub that grew on the left of the path. 'Some blackbirds have built their nest in this bush. I'm trying to put this wire up to stop the cats getting in. Only trouble is, I need four hands.'

' – Let me lend you a couple more.' Opening the gate he went through and between them they pulled open the roll of wire and circled the bush with it. He held it in place then while she secured the ends together with string. 'I don't know if it'll work,' she said, 'but it's worth a try.'

Standing above the bush he could see the nest as a darker mass deep in the midst of the foliage. When he looked up again she was smiling at him. She had a very open face. He didn't think she could be more than twenty-four or twenty-five.

'Thank you so much,' she said. She wiped her hands on her old jeans. 'And now what can I do for you?'

He shrugged. 'I was just driving by when I caught sight of you. And – I thought I'd stop and say hello . . .' He thought how crass his words sounded.

'Well – that's very neighbourly of you,' she grinned. 'And at such an opportune moment. I'm really very grateful. The blackbirds would be too – if they knew. Can I offer you a cup of tea in payment for your help?'

'Oh, no thank you. I can't stop. I've got a friend waiting in the car . . .'

'Well, perhaps some other time, then.'

'Yes, I'd like that.' He paused, then: 'I – I wanted to meet you,' he said. 'I've just been talking to Edith Carroll – your neighbour – and looking at her collection of pictures. And I saw your two paintings there.'

'Oh.' She nodded.

'And – well, I just – wanted to tell you how I admire your work.'

'Thank you.'

'I saw one of your paintings in one of the village shops, too. The one of the trees by the chalkpit . . .'

This time she just nodded. Her smile was still there but now it seemed less open, somehow less real. Hal was aware of a slight feeling of awkwardness – yet he persevered.

'I'd love to see some more of your work sometime,' he said. 'Would that be possible?'

'Oh, no, I'm afraid not. I don't have anything here. And you see, I don't paint anymore, so . . .' She shrugged. Her smile now seemed merely polite.

'You've stopped painting?'

'Yes. I haven't done any for a while now.'

He wanted to ask how such a thing could be; how she could own such a talent and not use it. After a moment he said: 'Well – maybe in the future – soon – you'll get back to it again.'

'Oh, no, it's quite finished with.' She dismissed the idea with a little shake of her head. Her smile came and went again, and then she sighed and said, 'Ah, well . . .' – clearly telling him that she couldn't stand around chatting.

'I won't keep you any longer,' he said. He felt foolish and was wishing now that he hadn't stopped. 'I can see you're busy, and besides, I'd better get back to my friend . . .' He moved to the gate, opened it and went through. As he closed it behind him Mary Hughes's eyes met his. Her smile was warm again now.

'Once more, Mr Graham,' she said, 'thank you for your help.'

Back in the car Alison looked at him with wry curiosity. 'Do you often do that?' she said, ' – just get out and go for a walk?'

'Sorry about that. But I wanted to have a word with Mary Hughes. She lives there – I suppose you know.'

'Yes, of course.'

When he made no attempt to start the car but just sat there looking ahead she asked him what he was so thoughtful about. He told her then of the meeting that had just taken place. Afterwards she said:

'And her manner changed just like that? – when you brought up the subject of her painting?'

'Yes. It was so obvious that she didn't want to talk about it.' He paused. 'I wonder what could have happened . . .'

' – Happened?'

'Well, something must have. She doesn't paint at all now. Something must have happened to bring that about.'

Alison nodded thoughtfully. 'Yes,' she said, ' – but she's different in other ways. It's not only with regard to her painting . . .'

'You know her?'

'I used to. When I first came here we met and became quite friendly. She was fairly new to the village as well then – so we had something in common. Of course she wasn't on her own then. Miss Larkin was there too.'

'Miss Larkin?' He had a sudden flashing vision of the woman on the edge of the chalkpit. He saw her leaping up, going over the edge. 'Mary Hughes was living with her?'

'As a paying guest. She'd come here to paint – from London.'

'When was that?'

'Oh – sometime after Christmas, I think. She – Mary – told me that she'd come with the intention of doing a series of Devonshire landscapes. Miss Larkin had a room to let – an extension like a studio at the back of the cottage. Mary took it. It suited her very well.'

'And you got friendly with her . . .'

'Yes, fairly. Mind you, she was pretty busy most of the time. She never seemed to think about much apart from her work. It was everything to her. When she wasn't up in her studio she'd be outside, sketching or taking photographs. Didn't matter what the weather was like – raining or snowing.'

'That makes it even more odd – her rejection of it all now.' He paused. 'So – what happened after she came here . . . ?'

'She stayed. Then, sometime in March old Miss Larkin went off her head.'

'She what?'

'Oh, yes. They shut her up in Primrose House. Though she got out one occasion. She came round to The Laurels, asking to see me.'

She'd got out on more than one occasion, Hal thought. *She'd got out and gone to the chalkpit and thrown herself over . . .* 'Did you see her?' he asked.

'Only for a few moments. I'd answered the door to her. She was in a terrible state. She wanted to talk to me, she said. She really looked quite – desperate.'

Alison's words thrust into his mind Miss Larkin's words to him: *But you've got to let me talk to you. You must listen to me.* 'What did she want to say?' he asked.

'I don't really know. She didn't have much of a chance to say anything. Miss Allardice was there within seconds – grabbing Miss Larkin and telling me to go and tell Miss Carroll. Miss Carroll got on the phone and the next thing, Miss Larkin was being taken away again.'

Hal waited. 'And then what?' he asked.

Alison shrugged. 'That was about it. Mary stayed in the cottage – where she is now – and Miss Larkin died. I think Miss Larkin must have left the place to her. She was very fond of her, I know.' Frowning, she added after a second: 'Mary changed after that. Now if we meet we just say hello and exchange a few words. Nothing more. Mind you, she's still very pleasant – but that's the way people are in Moorstone.'

Hal had made no attempt to start the car. They lit fresh cigarettes and he watched the smoke drift out into the light breeze. 'That whole thing,' he said, 'I find it rather – disturbing . . .'

'Miss Larkin and Mary Hughes? Yes, I know what you mean.' She paused then added quietly: 'But there's – something about this whole place that disturbs me. There's something phoney about it. And it's not only to do with Miss Larkin and Mary Hughes; they're just a part of it.'

'Go on.'

'I don't really know what I'm trying to say. I only know

that I'll be bloody glad when Geoff gets back.' She frowned and shook her head. 'Ah, listen to me. Take no notice. It's so – unfair of me to offer you *my* jaundiced feelings about the place. Enough, enough . . .' She opened her handbag and took out a folded piece of newspaper. 'Here,' she said as she handed it over, I found this. I thought it might be of interest to you.'

The page, torn from one of the dailies of a few months before, was mostly devoted to gossip and scandal. Near the centre was a photograph to which Alison pointed, saying, 'There he is – the previous owner of your house.'

So this was Lewis Childs. The picture showed a man of about forty-five, drunkenly smiling in the company of a flashy blonde with a vacuous smile who nestled close to his shoulder. Childs, a handsome man with square jaw and thick dark hair, was shown with one hand around a champagne glass and the other on the hand of his companion. Beneath the picture the caption read:

> Playboy and man-about-town Lewis Childs had reason to celebrate la dolce vita on Rome's Via Veneto the other night. Following his recent acquittal on charges of narcotics possession he is shown here relaxing with one of his newer interests. His smile was short-lived, however. Soon after the above photograph was taken he was involved in a fracas with other patrons for which he was consequently, and unceremoniously, ejected from the nightspot.

'Mm . . . not the kind of person I'd care to be close to,' Hal said as he handed the paper back to Alison. 'Can they be serious when they say he planned to return to Moorstone? It's hard to imagine. What could a person like that want to come back to a place like this for?'

'Yes, odd, isn't it? Particularly as he never came from the village in the first place.'

'He didn't?'

'No, by what I've heard he was one of those people who

came here from outside, and just – adopted the place as his home . . .'

Hal looked at her in silence for a moment, then he took a last drag from his cigarette and dropped it out of the window. Reaching down, he turned the key in the ignition.

'I think we'd better get going,' he said. 'Rowan will be wondering where we are.'

14

Soon after Hal and Rowan got back from seeing Paul Cassen on Monday morning Hal left for London. Mrs Palfrey saw him go.

Standing at the sitting-room window, duster in hand, she'd paused in her task of polishing the small walnut table and watched as he'd put his suitcase onto the back seat of the car and taken Rowan in his arms. After he'd kissed her he'd driven away. He would leave the car in Exeter and take the train from there, Rowan had told Mrs Palfrey. He wouldn't be returning till Wednesday.

Now Mrs Palfrey turned away from the window, put down the duster and went into the kitchen. She was filling the kettle at the sink when Rowan came in.

'I thought you might like a cup of coffee,' Mrs Palfrey said. They drank far too much coffee, the Grahams. It wasn't good. Still, a few more cups wouldn't hurt.

Rowan smiled at her. 'Lovely. Thank you.'

'How did you get on this morning?' Mrs Palfrey asked as she switched on the kettle.

'Oh, fine. Dr Cassen certainly seems to know what he's doing.'

'Yes, no doubt of that.' Mrs Palfrey paused. 'And how are you feeling today?'

'You mean that – sick feeling I had? Oh, fine. I don't know what was in the medicine Dr Cassen gave us but it certainly seems to have worked. For both of us.'

'That's good.'

'And my wrist is going on very well, too . . .'

'And there's no chance of any – permanent damage?'

'Good Lord, no. Another week or so, he says, and it'll be as right as rain. That'll be a relief, I can tell you. I shall be able to get on with some work again. It's such a nuisance being hampered in this way.' Rowan picked up her bag and moved towards the door. 'Well – I'd better go and change.'

'Your coffee will be ready in a minute or two. I'll bring it in to you.'

Rowan smiled from the doorway. 'You know, I'm going to miss all this once my wrist is better. You're spoiling me dreadfully.'

She went away then and Mrs Palfrey got on with the business of making the coffee. When the tray was ready she carried it into the sitting room. Rowan, now wearing a blouse and jeans, was using her left hand to continue the polishing where Mrs Palfrey had left off. She was singing as she worked. Breaking off her song as Mrs Palfrey entered she said over her shoulder, 'I can't use my typewriter, but this is something I *can* do. I must do something. I can't just sit around.'

Mrs Palfrey put her head on one side and gave her a little admonishing look. 'Well, just so long as you don't overdo it.'

She set the tray down and poured the coffee. Rowan came and sat on the sofa. Her blouse had short sleeves and Mrs Palfrey noticed at once the small, round sticking-plaster in the crook of her left elbow.

'Have you hurt yourself again?' she asked.

'What? Oh, that. No, not at all!' Rowan laughed. 'My God, you're making me sound like a walking disaster area! No, that's just where Dr Cassen took some blood for one of his tests.' She paused and added with a grin, 'He didn't take only blood, either. If nothing else, one has to admit that he's thorough. God, but I hate those needles and things.'

'You poor thing. And Mr Graham – he had the same tests?'

'Oh, yes. Why should I be the only one to suffer!'

Mrs Palfrey left her then and returned to the kitchen where

she took her handbag from her shopping basket. Opening the bag she took out a worn and crinkled, unsealed envelope. From inside that she pulled out a flimsy twist of tissue paper. Placing it on the table she opened it out and looked at the bits of dried leaves, petals and berries that lay there. After a moment she threw the envelope into the trash-bin, wrapped the bits in the paper again, put it into her pocket and went outside.

As she walked down the path between the cabbages and the beans she glanced over to her right and saw Tom Freeman emerging from the garden shed with a rake in his hand. Seeing her he gave a short wave and she came to a stop and shot him a brief look, wide-eyed and eyebrows raised. Then, as he stared at her she moved her right hand and touched her fingertips to the inside of her left elbow. It was just the briefest gesture. He smiled slowly and then formed his mouth into a single, silent word:

'*Both . . . ?*'

Mrs Palfrey nodded, turned away and moved on along the path.

As she drew closer to the orchard she looked around and saw that the old man was following her. She stopped when she came to the patch where all the plants grew wild in their rich, strange-scented profusion. Freeman came to her side and watched as she took the twist of paper from her apron pocket.

'When?' he said.

'This morning.'

His slow nod was all satisfaction. He watched as she opened the paper. 'So there's no more need for that stuff anymore.'

'Let's hope not.'

'And they're all right, are they?'

'All right?'

'They're feeling all right . . .' He paused, then added awkwardly: 'You didn't overdo it . . .'

'Of course not,' she snapped. 'It needed hardly anything. Just enough to put them off colour for a few days – and get them to the doctor.' She looked at him scornfully. 'How on earth would you manage on your own? You'd be useless.'

'I've managed in the past,' he said defensively.

She shrugged. 'I suppose you must have.' She smiled then, and went on: 'You should see her in there. Happy as a lark. I've never seen her like it before.' She laughed. 'And extolling the virtues of Dr Cassen's medicine. So much enthusiasm for a bit of coloured water.' Opening the twist of paper she leaned forward and shook it so that the bits of dry plant fell scattered amongst the fresh green. Turning back to the old man and seeing the satisfaction in his eyes she said, with a malicious little note of assumed sadness:

'But now *he's gone . . .*'

' – What?'

'He's gone. He's not happy here. He's left. Gone back to London . . .'

His mouth fell open in dismay and he stared at her in wide-eyed panic. '*Gone – ?*'

'As soon as they got back from seeing Cassen.' He shook his head. His expression now was all horror. '*No,*' he groaned. 'You don't mean that.'

She continued to look at him for a moment or two, then she relented.

'No,' she smiled. She'd enjoyed his agony. 'He's coming back – in two or three days.'

His eyes closed momentarily in relief, and he said, 'Oh . . .' on a long, deep sigh. Then, giving her a reproving shake of his head he said, 'Don't do that to me, Sylvia.'

She chuckled. 'You believed me, didn't you? – for a second there? I really had you on the run.' Still chuckling, she screwed up the bit of tissue paper and thrust it into her pocket. Then, her expression serious again, she added: 'But it's true: he's *not* happy here. I can tell. And if it's left up to him I don't think they'd be likely to stay that much longer.'

She and the man looked silently at one another for a few moments, then she turned and made her way back towards the house.

15

Miss Carroll was bent over her desk, writing. After a few moments she looked up and smiled. 'You're off now, are you?' she said.

Alison nodded. 'If that's all right with you?'

'Of course, my dear. What time is your appointment?'

'Eleven forty-five.'

'Fine, then you run along. Did you phone your friend Mrs Graham?'

'Yes. We're going to meet for lunch when I come out. You're sure you're not going to need me . . .'

'Quite sure. And don't bother about hurrying back; there'll be nothing for you to do today.' She sighed, turned in her chair and looked at the pile of manuscript pages on her desk. 'This should be the best thing I've ever done. It's a shame that that husband of yours has to go and upset my plans. Still, it can't be helped.' Looking back at Alison she smiled briskly. 'Well, off you go. Go and get yourself looking pretty for when he gets here.'

In the kitchen Alison told Miss Allardice that she wouldn't be in for lunch. Then she went up to her room, where she picked up her bag and made a quick check in the mirror. She had just got down to the hall again when the front doorbell rang. Opening the door she saw Ralph Collins standing on the porch, his burly frame cutting out the light. Anyone looking less like a librarian was, to her mind, hard to imagine.

'Miss Carroll's expecting me,' he said. The smile he gave her was too warm, too ingratiating. She made no attempt to return it but simply opened the door wider. He stepped through into the hall and stood there, blocking her exit. 'Off out, are you?' he said.

'Yes.'

'Shall you be joining us for lunch?'

'No.' She kept her distance and didn't look at him.

'Couldn't you be persuaded to join us?'

'Not by you.' She glared at him and then looked away again. She hated his florid, freckled complexion, his wiry, red hair. Taking a small step forward she said, 'Would you excuse me. I'm going to be late.'

He didn't move. 'Please,' he said, his voice low, ' – we just got off to a rather bad start, that's all.'

'We haven't got off to *any* start. And that's the way I intend to keep it.'

'You know,' he said, 'I'm really not such a bad fellow. Couldn't we get together for a friendly little chat sometime? Get to know one another?'

'No, I'm sorry.'

'You're not sorry at all.'

'No, I'm not.' She shook her head in exasperation. 'Mr Collins, why don't you give up? You know there's no point in all this. I've made it quite clear to you how I feel, and I'm damned certain that with my husband arriving in just a few days I'm hardly likely to change my attitude now. Not that I *ever would*.' She took another step forward. Still he didn't move.

Giving her a slow smile, he said, 'I'll bet you've got a fantastic body.'

Turning abruptly, she stepped away along the hall, knocked on Miss Carroll's study door and opened it. 'Mr Collins is here,' she announced. On hearing the old lady's reply she looked back to the man. 'Miss Carroll's waiting for you now.'

'What time will you be back?' he asked as he came towards her.

'With any luck, after you've gone.'

Without looking at him again she stepped past him to the front door. As she closed it behind her she breathed a sigh of relief. And with more luck, that would be the last she'd see of him. After Sunday there wouldn't even be the risk of her setting eyes on him again.

*

They were in the restaurant of The Swan, sitting at one of the tables overlooking the High Street. Alison was eating steak. Rowan, still one-handed, had opted for an easy-to-manage beef stroganoff. Beyond the net-curtained window they could see the villagers going by on the pavement. Alison hadn't told Rowan her news over the phone; now, though, she did.

'But you said he wasn't due for almost another three weeks,' Rowan said.

'No, he wasn't. But now his plans have changed.' With a sudden wide smile Alison added excitedly, 'Just *five days*! Five days and Geoff'll be back in England! I can hardly believe it!'

'When did you hear?'

'Just this morning.'

'And Miss Carroll knows?'

'Oh, yes. She's taking it surprisingly well, all things considered. She was quite thrown at first, I could tell, but – she's being very nice about it all. Very understanding.'

'Is that why you've had your hair done – because of Geoff?'

Alison shrugged. 'I don't really want to look a mess when he gets here.' She reached up and touched at her hair. It was a little shorter now. The ends curved up just below her ears. 'It does look better, doesn't it?' she said.

'Oh, yes, it does.' Rowan nodded. 'Did you get it done here in the village?'

'Yes, just along the High Street. I was a bit anxious at first but Miss Carroll assured me they were perfectly professional and, as she put it, "up to date." It was her idea that I had it done. Well, it had got a bit – straggly; she was right.' She shook her head. 'I suppose I haven't bothered that much while I've been here. Now, though, I have an incentive again.' Her hand went once more up to her hair. 'I think they did a good job, too. And they were very attentive. I think Miss Carroll must have told them to give me the royal treatment. She was the one who made the appointment for me.'

'She seems to be taking your departure very well.'

'Oh, yes, she is. She's even suggested that Miss Allardice drive me into Exeter so that I can do some shopping; get some new clothes. I might go. I don't know yet.' She grinned. 'Not much time, is there?'

'No, there isn't. Have you got everything planned?'

'Sort of. Geoff should get here sometime Sunday after-noon. I thought I'd book a room for us here for that night and then – we leave for London on the Monday. We'll stay in London till we fly out. He's got business meetings to attend and there's also my visa and things like that to be sorted out.'

'It's all happening so quickly.'

Alison laughed. 'Yes, that's what Miss Carroll said.' She took a sip from her wine glass; shook her head. 'I've no idea whether she's done anything about finding anyone to replace me, but – oh, well, I'm sure she's got it all taken care of. I don't like leaving her in the lurch but – I'm afraid I'm just being very selfish. All I can think about is the fact that Geoff's coming back. Not even that persistent bastard Collins could put me off my stroke today.'

'Is he still acting up?'

'He tries. Ah, but why talk about him on such a lovely day. How's your stroganoff?'

'Very good, thanks.'

'You seem to be coping very well. How is the wrist?'

'Coming on. Few more days and I'll be able to use it prop-erly again. It hasn't been too bad, though. And thank God for Mrs Palfrey. She's been a great help. A little too much some-times – the way she fusses over me; but her heart's in the right place.'

There was something different about Rowan today, Alison thought. There was an effervescence about her; a carefree quality that she hadn't noticed before.

'You know, you're looking so much better,' Alison said.

'Oh, I *feel* better. I feel great. Paul Cassen's good, isn't he? – and you were right about his being thorough.' Rowan then went on to tell of the checkup she and Hal had been given the day before. 'I thought Paul would just take our blood pres-sure,' she said. 'Not a bit of it; he took our blood.' Lowering her voice she added, 'Not to mention urine specimens.'

Alison nodded. 'Same with me when I went to see him.'

'I know Hal regarded the whole thing as a damned nuisance,' Rowan went on, ' – but it's good to know that you're healthy, isn't it?'

'Have you heard from Hal?'

'He phoned last night.' Rowan frowned. 'He was so pleased to be there – in London. You could tell.'

'Why, what did he say?'

'It wasn't so much what he said. You could just hear it in his voice.'

'Well . . .' Alison shrugged, ' – he's still settling in.'

'Fine, but how much time does he need?'

But then Rowan's smile was back again; this time a little wistful, though, as she said, 'So, on Monday you'll be leaving Moorstone, and two weeks later you'll be in Saudi Arabia – making friends with all those other ex-patriate wives and going to all those illegal drinking parties. I've heard what it's like.'

'Oh, no, that's not my scene at all. Nor Geoff's.'

There was a little silence. Rowan said:

'I know we haven't known one another long, but – I shall miss you.'

'I shall miss you too. But look, let's keep in touch. Then when Geoff and I come back on leave or whatever we can meet. Let's not lose contact.'

'No, let's not.'

Later, after dessert, the waitress brought coffee. Alison added cream and sugar to hers and lit a cigarette. Glancing from the window she said with a nod:

'Oh, there's your friend. Two of your friends.'

Rowan leaned forward and looked out. David Lockyer was standing at his front gate talking to Mrs Palfrey, who held a shopping basket in her hands.

Alison grinned. 'Oh, she's getting her kicks, all right.'

'Mrs Palfrey? What do you mean?'

'I'm sure she's got the hots for him.'

Rowan laughed. 'You're making that up.'

'No, I'm not.'

'But – she's so much older than he is.'

'So? Since when have people been too old to make idiots of themselves?'

'But what makes you say that – about them?'

'I've watched them. On the few occasions I've accompanied Miss Carroll to church I've watched them – those two. Mrs Palfrey stands next to him in the choir. And she's so *attentive*. You can tell just by looking at her that she thinks the sun shines out of his eyes. And after all, they do have a common interest – their music.'

'Yes, I know, but – you don't think he's attracted to her, do you?'

'I'd hardly think so. No, he probably regards her as some nice, motherly old duck.'

Rowan nodded. 'Mm. I suppose Mrs Palfrey must get lonely at times – and it must be nice when some kind, handsome young man shares your own interests.'

'He is handsome, isn't he?'

'Oh, yes. And kind.' Rowan paused. 'He phoned yesterday – to ask how I was.'

'There's considerate for you.'

'Don't read anything into it. He's just a very nice man.'

Alison looked back to the window. Mrs Palfrey was moving away now, turning, beaming over her shoulder at Lockyer. 'Yes, and quite obviously Mrs Palfrey thinks so too.'

A little while later the two women paid the bill and got up from the table. Rowan must get back, she said, while Alison said she'd take the opportunity to book the room for herself and Geoff. They said goodbye in the foyer, Rowan going out onto the street and Alison turning to the reception desk where she rang the bell. When the landlord, Ian McBride, appeared – a tall, good-looking elderly man with a moustache – she asked him whether he had a double room available for the coming Sunday night. With a wide smile he told her that she could just about take her pick; they had very few clients there at the moment.

After reserving the room she turned towards the main door where an elderly couple was just coming in off the street. Alison held the door for them while they entered, then went out onto the pavement. There she stood wondering what to do. She didn't particularly want to go back to The Laurels just yet – especially as Collins was likely to be still there . . .

She was still debating her course of action when she became aware of the old couple emerging from the hotel and coming towards her. As they approached the old man gave her a diffident smile. He walked with a pronounced stoop; he had sparse grey hair and a plain, gentle face. At his side the old woman held on to his arm.

'Excuse me,' the man said, ' – can you tell me whether there's another hotel in the village?' His accent sounded northern.

'There's the Old Forge on School Lane . . .'

He shook his head. 'We've already tried there. It's full.'

'Full?' Alison turned and gestured to the doors of The Swan. 'And don't you fancy this place?'

'Oh, that's full up too.' He sighed. 'Well, we'll just have to go on and try to find somewhere else. Shame . . .' He briefly explained then that he and his wife were on a short motoring holiday – taking it very easy, he added – and had heard how attractive Moorstone was. 'So we thought we'd like to stay here for a few nights. It's such a nice, quiet little place.' Resignedly he added, 'Ah, well . . .'

He thanked Alison then and wished her goodbye, and she watched as he and the woman moved to an old Ford standing at the kerb. She remained standing there as it drew away and eventually disappeared round the bed of the High Street.

Why, she wondered, had Ian McBride turned them away? The hotel wasn't full; he'd told her as much himself.

Such a nice little place, Moorstone, the old man had said. Yes – that's how it had seemed to her when she'd first come here. She'd been so lucky to get the job, she'd thought then; after all, Moorstone was small and space for outsiders was limited. Now, though, thinking of the old couple's rejection, she found herself wondering at the nature of Moorstone's exclusiveness.

She turned and began to move away. David Lockyer in his little front garden was tending a rose tree. He glanced up as she passed by and gave her a neighbourly nod. She returned the nod and walked on, taking in the other neat houses and the modest-looking displays in the shop windows. She looked, too, at the familiar faces of the villagers. The vicar, Endleson, came past, murmuring a 'good afternoon,' his smile very bright against his unseasonal suntan. She saw Miss Banks, the tall, elegant headmistress of the village school; Woodson, the butcher, large and jolly; Marriatt, the vet with hair at his temples like white wings . . . The smiling, beautiful people of Moorstone . . . And they *were* beautiful, most of them. The young men were nearly all tall and handsome, the young women slim and pretty. And even the older folk, generally, still boasted evidence of handsomeness in their youth. She thought again, with sorrow, of the old couple. As regards their looks they'd never have been able to compete in Moorstone.

When she came to the spot where School Lane branched off to the right she crossed over to the other side. In the window of a shop opposite she watched her reflection appear. The sight of her newly-trimmed hair took her by surprise – she had quite forgotten about it. It did look much better, she thought; she was glad she'd taken Miss Carroll's advice.

She moved on along School Lane, leaving the main part of the village behind her. Soon, she would be leaving it behind her for good. Forever. She was glad.

A cold wind had sprung up and she buttoned the front of her light linen jacket. Looking over to the right she caught sight of the Stone. Briefly she shivered.

16

When Rowan had finished dressing after her bath Mrs Palfrey helped her do her hair. Rowan was pleased with the result. Having only one completely useful hand – and the wrong one at that – she'd found it a difficult job on her own.

She was due to leave soon for a few hours' shopping in Exeter with Alison. Miss Allardice was going to drive them in Miss Carroll's old Daimler.

Now Mrs Palfrey gave a final touch to Rowan's hair and then stepped back, looking admiringly with her head on one side. 'It looks very nice,' she said.

'Thanks to you.'

'What time is Mrs Lucas calling for you?'

'At ten-thirty.'

'Ah, well, you have a little time yet . . .'

Mrs Palfrey started on Rowan's fingernails then. After trimming them she began, carefully, to paint them with transparent lacquer. 'You have beautiful hands, you know,' she said.

Rowan smiled. 'Well – thank you.' After a pause she added, 'It's really so kind of you to do all this for me, Mrs Palfrey.'

'Don't mention it,' Mrs Palfrey told her; 'it was no trouble at all.' Then: 'Will you be back before Mr Graham returns?' she asked.

'He's not coming back till tomorrow. He phoned last night. He's got some more business there to attend to.'

When Mrs Palfrey had finished she looked down at Rowan's hands and nodded. 'You do have beautiful hands. They're lovely.' Then, with a little shake of her head she added, frowning, ' – Not like these old things of mine. They really let me down, you know.'

'You mean – your music . . . ?'

'Yes.' Releasing Rowan's hands she held her own higher. 'Arthritis is hereditary, you know. Well, so I'm told.'

'Is it?'

'Yes. Not that you'll have to worry about such a thing; at least I hope not, for your sake.'

'Oh, I hope not.'

'Did either your mother or your father suffer from it?'

'No, I'm sure they didn't.'

'Then you should be all right. You shouldn't have anything to worry about.'

After she'd spoken Mrs Palfrey got up from the bed where she'd been sitting and crossed to the window. She stood there gazing out. Rowan watched her in silence for a few moments then said quietly:

'Hal told me – about your career . . .' She shook her head. 'What – what rotten luck for you . . .'

'Yes, it was – rotten luck. It was my whole life – my music. And it all just – stopped. I couldn't go on with it. That's when I came back here, to Moorstone.'

'You must miss it a lot – your music – the performing . . .'

'Oh, yes.' She turned back to face Rowan. 'I did. I still do. For a few years I was still able to play at times – for my own amusement – when my hands weren't too bad. I had a – a special friend here in the village. A composer. Edwin Leclerc. He was my salvation. He even wrote music for me. Not that I could play it very well. In the end I couldn't play it at all.' She looked down at her hands and added bitterly: 'And about the most delicate job they're capable of now is trimming some-body's fingernails.'

Rowan was silent for a moment, then, attempting to move the conversation onto a less painful subject, she said: 'So there are two composers in Moorstone . . .'

'Two?'

'Well – with David Lockyer as well . . .'

Mrs Palfrey gave a little smile and shook her head. 'David Lockyer? No, he's the only one now. Leclerc is dead.' She paused. 'David Lockyer and Edwin Leclerc – they were great friends, you know. Lockyer is a talented young man. Quite brilliant. But he wouldn't be doing what he does today were it not for Leclerc. He owes everything to him.' She stood for a moment, obviously deep in thought. Then she shrugged. 'Ah, well,' she said, 'I mustn't stand here all day.' She smiled at Rowan. 'Is there anything else I can do for you?'

'No, nothing, thank you. You've been a great help.'

After Mrs Palfrey had gone Rowan sat for a moment idly looking at her reflection in the glass. Turning, glancing at the clock, she saw that it was almost ten twenty-five. Alison would be here at any minute. She got up, put on her shoes, picked up her bag and went out onto the landing.

Outside the next bedroom she came to a stop, hovered for a moment, then opened the door and went in.

She stood and looked around her. The room had once been a nursery. The wallpaper was patterned with animals, birds and butterflies.

And it could be a nursery again, she said to herself. It would be, sometime. And perhaps that time wasn't too distant. There was still no sign of her period, and now it was a week overdue. Seven days. Each day she'd expected it to appear and each day had come and gone without it.

Hal hadn't noticed at all. But he seemed so preoccupied lately. The fact of her lateness had just passed him by. And she hadn't mentioned it. She hadn't dared to. She hadn't dared acknowledge the growing hope within her.

Now, though, she did. Now, standing there in the empty room, she was suddenly aware that her hope had grown into a certainty.

17

Arriving at Paddington on Monday afternoon Hal had gone straight to his club near Marble Arch. He spent that evening having dinner with an old friend, one who – like all his other friends – he had not seen since giving up the London flat. The move to Moorstone had cut him off from them all, completely.

The following morning, Tuesday, he went to the British

Library to do some research for his book. The information he sought could just as easily have been found in the Moorstone library, he was sure, but that particular place did nothing at all for him. How, he asked himself, could its atmosphere compare with the atmosphere of *this* place – this great round room with its long rows of tables arranged in a sun-ray pattern? It wasn't only that, though. . . .

When the time came – and it had passed so quickly – he closed his notepad and set off to meet Tim Farson, his agent. There in the office he sat for a couple of minutes while Farson completed a telephone call and then together the two men went out onto the street. Walking along High Holborn Hal limited his usually long stride to keep pace with the slower man. Farson had contracted polio as a child and had been left with a pronounced limp.

The restaurant, in an alley off the main street, was attractive and pleasant. The food was excellent and over the ensuing talk Hal experienced again that old excitement that always came from discussing his craft and the general business of selling books. Most important, though, he learned that Albert Goldman, who was to produce the film of *Spectre at the Feast*, was due in London for a brief visit, arriving on Thursday morning. 'He wants to know whether you'll be available to discuss the screenplay,' Farson said. 'I told him I felt sure you would be.' Hal nodded. Yes, of course; he'd phone Rowan and tell her he'd be staying on another night . . .

When the two men parted outside the restaurant Hal made his way without haste to Trafalgar Square and spent a couple of hours in the National Gallery. Afterwards he phoned Rowan and then bought a ticket for the evening performance of a new play with Glenda Jackson. Tomorrow he might go to the Tate or look around some of the Bond Street galleries. He was back in the town he loved, but the way he was cramming in his experiences made him feel like a tourist.

That night he lay in his bed in the club and thought of the day past. He thought, too, of Rowan in the peace and quiet of Crispin's House. How different from here. From along the corridor echoed the sound of a clanging lift gate, while out-side on the street the traffic never ceased its moving. In a few minutes he was asleep.

On Thursday morning after breakfast Tim Farson phoned to say that Goldman was tied up in New York and wouldn't be arriving in London as planned. 'Though he does hope to make it sometime over the next few days,' he added. ' – I'll keep you posted. Sorry to mess you around like this.'

'Oh, that's okay,' Hal said. It was; he'd had an extra day in London; an extra day away from Moorstone.

'So you'll be going back home now, will you?' Farson asked.

'After lunch, I should think . . .'

'And would you be able to get back up here again at fairly short notice?'

There was no doubt about it. 'Yes, of course,' Hal said.

Leaving the club he strolled among the shoppers on Oxford Street, visited a couple more private galleries, then bought a paper and found a little café where he sat at a window table and drank coffee. He felt very far away from Moorstone.

And then, suddenly, on one of the inner pages of the news-paper his eye was caught by a familiar name. He read the words *Lewis Childs Making Progress*, and then beneath:

> Lewis Childs is said to be making good progress following his car accident of a month ago. A spokesman for the Milan hospital in which the wealthy playboy has been under intensive care said yesterday that Mr Childs's health has much improved and that, hopefully, he would soon be discharged. The extent of Mr Childs's injuries was not disclosed, though it was stated that he has undergone a series of major surgical operations.

Hal closed the paper and laid it on the table. It was ironic; even here in the heart of London's West End he couldn't, it seemed, get away from reminders of Moorstone.

After he'd ordered more coffee he lit a cigarette and watched the people going by on the sunlit pavement; the white, the black, the brown and the yellow, the prosperous and the down-and-outs, the healthy and the sick, the beautiful and the ugly, the ordinary and the bizarre – he had almost forgotten what an assortment London was made of. All of life was here, and he realized how much he had missed being a part of it all.

The café had become crowded, and glancing around he noticed a young couple standing in the doorway looking hopelessly at the occupied tables. The young man had only one arm. Hal got up and moved out into the sun. He'd get back to the club, have an early lunch and go to the station. He'd catch the three twenty-five – which would get him to Exeter about six o'clock.

Easing himself up against the pillows he switched on the bedside lamp. In its soft, mellow glow he turned and looked at Rowan beside him. Her head was turned away from him on the pillow. Leaning over slightly he saw that she was asleep.

Propping his own top pillow against the head-board he lit a cigarette and leaned back. He could find no rest at all. He looked at the clock. Just after one-fifteen. His eyes felt prickly from his efforts to close them and relax, and he was further from sleep than ever.

When his cigarette was finished he stubbed it out and then, very gently and slowly so as not to wake Rowan, got out of bed. After putting on his dressing gown he switched off the lamp and, by the faint light of the moon that came through the parted curtains, went quietly out of the room.

In the kitchen he made tea, poured it into a mug and went back up to the bedroom. He sat there in the small soft chair by the window, smoking, drinking the tea and looking out into the night.

It was so still. Everything seemed so serene, so untroubled. A faint breeze came, trembling the silvered leaves of the beech tree and moving the curtain at his side. Beyond the village he could see, rising up, the dark shape of the Stone. Between, in the hollow, the houses of the village were hardly discernible.

They looked to be asleep; he could see no lights there.

Why, he asked himself, could he not rest in this place? He recalled again how, sitting in the train bound for Exeter, he had found himself approaching his destination with dismay and a strange, inexplicable feeling of disquiet. What was it about this place that bred in him such negative emotions? For it was *this place* that did it. One thing he was sure of now – it wasn't just life in a small country village that he couldn't come to terms with; it was life in Moorstone. It was simply that.

He realized now that he never had settled; had never been close to it from the first moment. Strange, for all his anxiety in the beginning had been for Rowan; he had been so concerned for her happiness. It was for that reason that he had dreaded her learning of Miss Larkin's suicide on the day of their arrival. And it had been kept from her – while he had lived with the unfading memory of the horrific happening.

But it wasn't only the death of Miss Larkin that stood in the way of his contentment here. There was more to it than that. But what? He thought of Alison saying of the villagers: 'They're perfect, all right. They're too damn perfect,' and a little later her startling news that there was a mental home in the village. Hitherto subconscious pictures came leaping to the fore, and he thought again of Tim Farson limping beside him along the London street. He recalled too the one-armed young man who had stood in the café doorway. . . .

But why should he think of them? Why had the thought of their disabilities remained in his mind? He sighed. Everything in his mind was confusion. Nothing seemed to make sense anymore.

Turning in his chair he looked across at the bed. Rowan's body was just a dim, shadowy shape. He recalled her mood when he'd returned to the house this evening – so bright, so happy and contented. He hadn't seen her like that – so completely joyous – in a very long time. It seemed that even Alison's impending departure – of which Rowan had told him – couldn't dampen her spirits today.

He had managed to do it, though.

Witnessing her happiness he had found himself sinking deeper into his own despondency – and he'd become totally uncommunicative. Cruelly he'd refused to respond positively to the lightness of her mood, and in the end the two of them had lapsed into a polite quietness. He'd watched it happen, yet there had been nothing he could do about it; nothing he would do about it . . .

Finally, around nine o'clock, Rowan had murmured something about being tired and had gone to bed. Coming into the bedroom himself some two or three hours later he had found her sleeping soundly. Standing above her, looking down at her shadowed face, he'd realized the cause of his present mood. He resented her happiness at being in this place. And he resented, too, the fact that she had brought him here.

18

When Rowan awoke the next morning Hal was still asleep at her side.

Quietly, so as not to disturb him, she got out of bed and without putting on her dressing gown went into the bathroom.

She dropped the used tampon into the lavatory bowl, flushed it away and took a fresh one from the cabinet. Her head ached. After she'd showered she took two Paracetamol tablets. She was running true to her usual pattern now; the headache, she knew, would soon go away. It was the only thing in the way of pain that ever accompanied her periods. It was the least part of her discomfort right now.

After she'd brushed her teeth she sat on the bathroom stool with her hands clasped in her lap. She didn't want to go back to the bedroom. She didn't want to face him.

Yesterday she had waited so eagerly for his return from London. She'd known all day that she'd tell him as soon as she could; she'd have to; she couldn't keep it to herself. But the right time for telling him had never come. He'd been morose

and preoccupied, responding to her questions about his trip
with answers that were little more than curt phrases – which
in turn had become monosyllables. He had shown no interest
in anything. She had told him that Alison's husband was due
to arrive on Sunday and that she, Rowan, had invited them for
dinner on that day. Did he, Hal, have any other plans? No, he'd
briefly told her, he had not. She had then tried to gain a more
positive response by telling him of her conversation with Mrs
Palfrey when the old lady had reminisced about her past and
the man Leclerc. Nothing, though, had been able to draw him
out of his quiet preoccupation. They had eaten dinner almost
in silence, and the Good News with which she had earlier been
brimming over she had kept to herself.

As it had turned out, she now thought, it was as well that
she had.

It was very soon after that dinner that she had suddenly
realized, with horror, what was happening within her body.
Quickly then she had left him and come upstairs, there discovering that the blood was already staining the inside of her
jeans. For a long time she'd just stood in the bathroom and
wept, leaning forward, face bent low, clutching the side of the
wash-basin. Her mouth wide open, ugly, she had been racked
by her sobs.

Afterwards, in bed, she'd taken two sleeping tablets. She
hadn't used such things for ages – but she didn't want to be
awake when he came up . . .

Now she rose from the stool and went back into the bedroom.
It was almost seven-thirty. He lay with his eyes closed. She got
dressed as quietly as she could. Moving back to the bed she
reached out to pick up her wristwatch and his hand came out
and closed over her arm. Not looking at him she remained
quite still. After a moment he pulled her down so that she was
sitting on the bed. Then his other hand came up and around
her body.

'Please,' she said as she moved his hand away, 'don't touch
me.'

Without looking back she got up and went from the room.

19

Tom Freeman straightened above the herbaceous border, stretching the old, tired muscles in his back. Time was catching up on him; it was on the point of overtaking. This garden was too much for a man of his years. Not that *they* were aware of that – and they wouldn't be, either. As far as *they* knew the work was well within his capabilities. But there, what, with their limited experience, did they know? He'd convinced them, all right – at the beginning when they'd expressed doubts as to whether he was up to the work. He'd persuaded them that he was ideal. Well, he certainly had the necessary experience – and as for the physical requirements, well, he could fool them there for a while longer.

He stood still, catching his breath. There was a sharp pain in his lower back. He must have pulled a muscle on Wednesday when doing that heavy spade-work by the rockery. It was his own fault; he'd chosen to do it. This morning it had taken all his effort and will-power to drag himself out of bed.

He looked at his watch. Two-thirty. Not long to go now, then he could get off home and rest. Come Monday he should be feeling a lot better. Just as long as he could keep going for a while longer; then it would all be over and he could relax.

Hearing footsteps on the path he turned and saw Mrs Palfrey coming from the direction of the house. She was walking quite quickly, and after a glance at her face he stepped forward to meet her. She said as she drew near:

'Mrs Graham's asked me to tell you that you're wanted on the phone.'

'Do you know who it is?'

'No.' She turned and started off back along the path. He caught up with her.

'Who's in the house?'

'Only her – with a face like a wet week.'

'Didn't he get back – from London?'

'Yes. Sometime yesterday evening. He's gone out again now, though. All quiet and tight-lipped. I don't think things are going too well with them today.'

'Why's that? Have you any idea?'

'None at all.' She stopped and turned towards him. 'I was up in his study just now – after he'd gone. He had the morning paper open on his desk. He'd left it there . . . *The Times* . . .'

'Yes . . . ? So what?'

'It was open to the property page . . . flats and houses in London.' She paused. 'I told you: he doesn't like it here. He's not happy.'

She turned away again and moved off. When they got to the back door of the house she stopped in the doorway and gestured to his feet.

'Don't you come tracking a lot of dirt onto my clean kitchen floor.'

Dutifully he wiped his shoes on the coarse mat by the step and then followed her inside. She pointed to the telephone on the wall and he crossed to it and picked up the receiver.

'Hello – this is Tom Freeman. . . .'

'Tom?' the voice on the other end said, 'this is Jim Cleary.'

' – Oh, hello, Jim.' As he spoke the man's name he glanced across at Mrs Palfrey. She was standing by the sink, watching him; listening. Cleary's voice continued in his ear:

'I think you ought to call in here, Tom . . .'

'Oh – you mean today?'

'Of course today. As soon as you can.' Cleary paused. 'There's a certain somebody here right now. And it's the first time. God knows when he'll decide to come in again.'

'Right. I'll be there as soon as I can.'

'Well, it's up to you.'

'Yes, I'll be there. Thanks, Jim – you're a good friend. Oh, wait – listen – I don't want to go in while he's there.'

'His bike is outside so you'll easily know. I'd better go now; he's waiting.'

Tom Freeman thanked him again and hung up the receiver.

His hands trembled slightly. He turned to Mrs Palfrey. She was looking at him with a very faint little smile. As he moved towards the back door he saw Rowan approaching through the dining room. She was carrying an empty cup and saucer. She didn't look very happy, he thought; Mrs Palfrey was right.

'Did you get your phone call all right?' Rowan asked.

'Oh, yes, thank you, Mrs Graham.'

She nodded, put down the cup and saucer and started back.

'Oh, Mrs Graham – '

She stopped, turned towards him. 'Yes?'

' – We're going to need something for those darn slugs. They're getting at the lettuces.'

'Well – ' she shook her head helplessly, ' – do you know what to get for them?'

'Oh, yes. There're some pellets I could get. They'll do the trick.'

She nodded. 'Well, you get whatever you think is right and we'll settle up with you, as usual.'

'Fine. I might as well go and get the stuff now.'

'Whatever you think is best.' She looked as if she didn't want to be bothered.

When she had gone he said to Mrs Palfrey, shaking his head: 'God, I don't feel like walking into the village. My bloody back is killing me.' He sighed. 'Still, it's got to be done.'

'Oh, yes,' she said. Then she added, 'I'm already way ahead of you.'

He stopped; watched as she took up her handbag and withdrew from it a small change-purse. She beckoned to him with one finger and he went over to her. Out of the purse she took a little wad of Kleenex which she carefully opened and surreptitiously held up for his inspection.

'When did you get those?' he asked.

'On Wednesday.'

'How?'

'It was the easiest thing in the world. She can't do it herself, you see – not with her wrist like it is.' Her smile came again.

'Her accident – it could have been a disaster – but as it turned out it proved to be very fortunate – for me.'

'So it seems.'

He watched as she wrapped the nail-parings again and returned them to her purse, then he turned away, crossed to the door and left the house.

After collecting his jacket from the shed he set off towards the village. By the time he'd crossed over the river and turned left into the High Street he was already out of breath.

As he passed among the familiar faces of the villagers he realized how glad he'd be to see the last of them. He thought back into his past. Moorstone hadn't been the place for him then, and he'd got away from it was soon as he'd been able to. Many of the others were content to stay. Not he. Small, country villages were not for him; never had been; at least not to stay in for any length of time. While it served his purpose, though, he had to be content as well. Not long now and his purpose would be served, and he'd be away, on his travels. In his time he had travelled the world. That was the thing with him – travelling, discovering places he had never seen before. It was different nowadays, of course, when everyone trav-elled everywhere on their endless package tours. Today it was made much too easy; the fish-and-chips brigade turned up in the unlikeliest places. Yet none of them really knew what travelling was truly about. He did, though. And his chance had come again. Through his stertorous breathing he smiled. Not long now and he'd be off. That being so it would be goodbye to Moorstone – not forever, of course, but at least for a very long time.

As he drew closer to the barber's shop he looked across the street and saw the bicycle propped against a lamp post.

On his left was a small bookshop. He pushed open the door and went in. After giving a preoccupied nod to the proprietor – he knew him well – he stationed himself by the window, took up a book at random, opened it and stood watching the door on the opposite side.

It was almost five minutes before Hal emerged, got onto his bicycle and pedalled away along the High Street. Tom Freeman put the book down, went outside and looked off to the right. He could see Hal moving past The Swan towards the river; a few seconds later he was gone from sight. Without waiting any longer Tom Freeman hurried to the other side of the road and opened the door beneath the sign that said *James Cleary: Barber.*

Cleary smiled at him as he entered. He was a tall, heavy-set man with fair hair and a tanned, handsome face. 'I saw you across the street,' he said, 'going into Max Britton's shop . . .'

Tom Freeman nodded and wordlessly turned his attention to the floor around the hairdressing chair where bits of shorn, dark hair lay scattered on the linoleum. Cleary said:

'I swept the floor before I started so there's nobody else's there.'

'Fine. Thank you.'

'Did you know he was coming here today?'

'No idea. But how should I know?'

'Lucky you were there when I phoned, then.'

'I'll say. I'm grateful, Jim, I truly am.' He stood looking down at the bits of hair. There was relief in his expression.

'I'll get you something to put it in.' Cleary tore a paper towel from a roll and held it out to the old man. 'Or would you like me to do it?'

'No, no – I think it's better if I do it.' Tom Freeman took the towel from him, stooped and picked up several wisps of hair. Straightening again he folded up the paper into a neat little rectangle and put it carefully into his inside pocket. His face was pale.

'Are you all right?' Cleary asked a little anxiously.

'Just let me sit down a minute.' Tom Freeman walked to the worn leather bench by the wall and sat down.

'Would you like some water or something?'

'No, no, I'll be all right. Just let me sit here and get my breath.' He sat there with his hands hanging over the inside of his knees. 'I've had a few of these turns lately,' he said.

'You've probably been overdoing it.'

'There's no doubt about that.'

Cleary sat on the small padded stool next to the barber's chair. After a little silence he said, as if to fill the silence and make conversation: 'He's got a good head of hair.'

'Oh, I know.'

'Looks generally very healthy, too.'

'He is. We got the reports from the doctor. On both of them. Paul Gassen said they're both fine specimens.'

'That's nice to know. He – your man – Mr Graham – was telling me he'd been reading about Lewis Childs in the paper. You know about him, I suppose.'

Tom Freeman nodded. His breathing was a little easier now and his colour was returning. 'Shame about him,' he said. 'Haven't given him much of a chance, by what I've heard.'

'No, true, they didn't.'

'They *didn't?* Is it – different now?'

Cleary shrugged. 'It seems as though he's going to be all right. Didn't you read about it in the papers? He's recovering very well by all accounts. Coming out soon, I believe.'

Tom Freeman shook his head. 'I don't read the papers, and nobody's mentioned him to me. But why should they? I didn't know him. He was gone by the time I got back.' He sighed and got to his feet. 'Anyway, I'd better get off. I've got to buy some slug pellets too; I almost forgot.'

'How are you feeling now?'

'A bit better.' The old man moved to the door, gave Cleary a tired smile. 'Thanks again, Jim – for everything.'

'Don't mention it. We have to look after each other.'

'I'm grateful.'

Cleary smiled. 'Come and have a haircut before you leave us.'

Tom Freeman's smile grew momentarily brighter. 'Yes, I'll do that.'

He took his time getting back to Crispin's House. On the way he thought of what Jim Cleary had said about Lewis Childs. It gave him a slightly uneasy feeling in his chest.

When he got to the house he met Rowan just coming out into the yard. She gave him the hint of a smile as she asked:

'Did you get everything you wanted?'

'Yes, I did.' He nodded. 'Thank you.'

20

Just after noon on Saturday Hal was cycling along the High Street when he saw Alison emerge from one of the shops. He called her name and she looked around and smiled as he brought his bicycle to a stop at the kerb. 'Well, hello,' she said, 'and what are you up to?'

'Oh . . .' he shrugged, 'I've just been to the stationer's.'

'I see you've had a haircut, too.'

'Yesterday.'

'Very neat.' Indicating her shopping bag she added, 'I've just been getting a few things for Miss Carroll.'

'And have you finished?'

'The shopping? Oh, yes; there wasn't much to get.'

He gestured to The Swan across the street. 'Would you like a drink? – if you're not in a hurry . . .'

Following his glance she shook her head. 'Uh – no, thanks – not in that place. No, I think I'll head on back to The Laurels.' She paused, smiling. 'Tonight will be my last night there.'

'Geoff gets back tomorrow, so Ro tells me.'

'That's right.'

'And soon you'll be off for foreign climes. Exciting for you.'

'Oh, yes.'

'Look,' he said after a moment, 'I might as well walk back with you. I've got nothing much to do . . .'

'Okay, that'd be nice.'

He took her shopping bag, hung it over the handlebar and they set off along the High Street.

'What have you got against The Swan?' he said.

She hesitated for a moment and then told him about the elderly couple – the man and the blind woman – being refused accommodation there. 'And I know there was any number of rooms vacant,' she said. 'I know that because I'd only just booked up for Geoff and me. I wish now I'd gone to some other hotel – maybe in another village.' She shrugged. 'Still – it's done now.'

Her mention of the old couple struck a chord in him; he couldn't think what it was. Then as he pondered she went on:

'God, but this time is going slowly. You know, I'm just counting the hours till Geoff gets here. Silly, isn't it? But I can't help it.'

'What time do you expect to see him?'

'He phoned yesterday and gave me all the details of his flight and so on. We worked it out that he should be getting down here sometime after lunch – about half past two or three.'

'How will he get down here? By train?'

'No. He says he'll hire a car in London – and book a hotel for us while he's there.'

'If you went to London to meet him you'd save him all that journey.'

'Oh, I've got all my junk to get back. And apart from that I want you to meet him. By the way, it's still all right for dinner tomorrow, isn't it?'

'Oh, yes, I'm looking forward to it.'

'Good. I must phone Rowan in the morning and see what time she wants us. We left it rather up in the air.'

'What time will you be leaving Miss Carroll's?'

'As soon as Geoff arrives. I shall get all my things packed ready. Then we'll take it all straight over to The Swan. We'll leave for London the next morning, I suppose.'

On the subject of London she asked him how his recent trip had been. It had gone well, he told her, adding, after a pause: 'As a matter of fact – I didn't want to come back.'

She looked at him and shook her head. 'Oh, dear, that's a shame.'

'Yes, it is. But it's the truth.' He looked about him at the shops, the villagers going by about their business. 'There's just something about this place that – that doesn't suit me. It's good for Rowan, but it's not good for me. And it's not good for *us* – our relationship.'

'So – what are you going to do about it?'

He shrugged. 'I don't know. I wish I did. I keep telling myself it will pass – my feeling about it – Moorstone. Maybe it will, in time . . .'

She nodded. 'Yes, I expect so. You'll settle eventually.' With a smile she added, 'You'll see – you'll end up like all those other people.'

'What other people?'

'All those young people who come to Moorstone for a visit or something and end up staying, making it their home. They all seem to, don't they?' She paused. 'But here's one who won't. When I leave on Monday with Geoff that will be it.'

They turned from the High Street onto School Lane. After continuing in silence for a while Hal said:

'By "those young people" I suppose you mean Lewis Childs and Paul Cassen . . .'

'Yes. And Mary Hughes – and David Lockyer. And there might well be others I don't know about.'

He looked at her but said nothing. They came to the end of the houses and he gestured towards a five-barred gate over to the right. 'Would you like to stop for a cigarette?'

'I would indeed.'

After he'd propped his bicycle against the gate they lit cigarettes and leaned on the top bar. On the distant hill the shape of the Stone reared up, black against the sunlit hills beyond. Hal said:

'Paul Cassen told us that he was befriended by a doctor when he came here . . .'

'Yes. A Dr Richmond. He died in Primrose House.'

Hal looked at her.

'Yes,' she went on, '*and* Lockyer's benefactor. He was a composer – named Edwin Leclerc.'

'Rowan said something about him. Mrs Palfrey was telling her about him.' He paused. 'You say he *also* died in Primrose House?'

'Yes.'

'How do you know all this?'

'It's no secret. Besides, I've become . . . interested. I've asked a few discreet questions. And there's one thing I've come to realize . . .' She gave a strange, humourless little chuckle and added, 'I've come to realize that if you're a villager and befriend some young newcomer to the village you're quite likely to end up being committed.' She stared at him and then shrugged. 'Sounds insane, doesn't it? But that's what happened with Paul Cassen and Dr Richmond, Leclerc and Lockyer, and Mary Hughes and Miss Larkin.' A little silence fell, then she went on: 'There's a funny thing. You remember I was telling you about how Miss Larkin came round to The Laurels that day?'

'Yes?'

'She'd managed to get out of Primrose House, you remember. Well – in the short time while I was there with her at the front door – she called me Alison. Yet I'd never even really talked to her before. Why should she call me by my first name? And *why* – in the first place – did she come round asking for *me*?'

For the third night in a row he had found himself unable to sleep, and now once again he was at the bedroom window, gazing out over the shadowed village. In his hand was a cigarette; beside him a mug of tea, now swiftly cooling. Behind him in the bed Rowan was sleeping. Like last night and the night before she'd come to bed before him . . . This day past, like the previous one, had seen them no closer. Tonight, when he'd climbed into bed beside her she had briefly awakened and he'd nestled up to her warmth; he was tired of the tight-lipped silence that had prevailed since his return from London. But she had moved away from him. The movement of her body had been slight, the merest cold tightening, but it had been enough – enough to drive him back so that they no longer touched. Then, after an hour he had got out of bed to sit where he now was, looking out into the night. It was almost two o'clock.

He straightened suddenly in his chair. He could see a light

ahead. The tiniest pinpoint of light, up on the hill beyond the village. Then a second one appeared; then another, and another. In the end they were clustered there, moving slowly along the line of the hill to where the Stone rose up.

He sat watching as the lights moved up onto the rock itself and remained there, wavering, moving about, for at least an hour.

And then they vanished. Quickly, one by one, they all went out and he was looking into the unrelieved shadow again.

He shook his head as if to clear his brain. Then, stubbing out the remains of his cigarette he got up from the chair. He must try to sleep.

Throwing off his dressing gown he climbed into bed beside Rowan's stillness – but he lay apart from her; he wouldn't risk another rebuff. Sleepless, eyes open, he stared into the darkness.

Into his mind came the memory of what Alison had told him by the five-barred gate. He could remember how he had looked at her, shaking his head in bewilderment; it was all beyond him. 'Paul Cassen, David Lockyer and Mary Hughes,' he had said. 'Are you aware of what an incredible coincidence it all adds up to? They each come here from outside, get in with one of the villagers and end up staying on . . .'

'Right. While the particular villagers – their benefactors – end up dying in the nuthouse.'

'Jesus Christ,' he'd said after a moment. 'It's like some bloody sickness.'

21

It was almost eleven when Hal awoke. When he had showered and shaved he went downstairs and found Rowan in the kitchen preparing breakfast. He could hear the rather aggrieved tone in his voice as he said, 'You might have woken me – rather than let me sleep on.'

'I did call you once,' she said, 'but you didn't stir. So, as you were obviously tired I thought you might as well sleep a little longer. Did I do the wrong thing?'

He didn't answer. Rowan turned back to the stove, picked up eggs from a bowl and held one poised over the frying-pan. 'Are you ready to eat?' she asked.

'Yes, thank you.' He noticed then that her right wrist was bare. 'You got rid of your bandage,' he said.

'I took it off yesterday. Paul Cassen said I should if it felt okay.' She turned to him with the faintest smile. 'I thought as a writer you were supposed to be observant.'

'Mmm . . . I suppose I had that coming.' He returned her smile, just. 'And does it feel okay now?'

'Fine.' She nodded. 'It's perfectly all right.'

Just after three o'clock Rowan announced her intention of giving Alison a ring. 'She and Geoff ought to be back by now,' she said, 'and I've got to make sure they're coming tonight.' She had already spent some time in the kitchen making preparations for the dinner.

'They are coming,' Hal said. 'She told me yesterday.'

'Anyway, we've got to fix up a time . . .'

As she moved to the telephone Hal went up to his study where he sat looking out over the village. The sun was bright on the rooftops and on the Stone. Before him on his desk lay the file containing the results of his work on the novel. He hadn't touched it in days. Beside it lay *The Times*, open to the section advertising houses and flats for sale. He stared at it for a while then got up, paced the room for a minute or two and then went downstairs. He was just crossing the hall when the telephone rang. It would probably be Alison, he thought as he moved to answer it. But it was not Alison. It was Tim Farson, calling from his home in London.

The conversation was brief and when it was over Hal replaced the receiver and stood for a moment in thought. Then he went in search of Rowan. Not finding her in the house he looked from the sitting room's rear window and saw her in the garden. He went out to her.

She was sitting on the old wooden bench near the laburnum tree. She looked up as he approached.

'Was that Alison on the phone?' she asked.

'No, it was Tim Farson.'

'Oh.' She sounded disappointed. 'I couldn't get hold of her just now,' she said.

'What?'

'Alison. I couldn't reach her.'

'Oh.' He nodded, unconcerned. But Rowan was frowning.

'Miss Allardice answered the phone,' she went on. 'When I asked to speak to Alison she said she was too busy to come to the phone right then.'

'Well – she does have a husband who's just returned. And she hasn't seen him in a while, has she?'

'I *know* that. Even so . . .'

'So what did you do?'

'I asked her to get Alison to phone me as soon as she could – just to let me know about this evening. What else could I do?'

There was a pause, then Hal said: 'Uh . . . about this evening . . . I'm afraid there's a slight problem . . .'

'What's that?'

' – I've got to go up to London.'

'I see.' She paused. 'You've *got* to go?'

'Yes, I have to. I must.'

'When, exactly?'

'I told you – this evening. The producer of *Spectre* is arriving in London later today, and I've agreed to see him first thing tomorrow morning. I'll have to travel up tonight and stay at the club. There's nothing else for it.'

'But – Alison and Geoff are coming for dinner. You can't just – go off like that . . .'

'I'm sorry. I really am. But what else can I do? Goldman's only going to be in London for one day. He's going on to Rome tomorrow evening. We'll have a lot to talk about with the screenplay and not much time to do it in. Unless you'd rather I flew out to the States and talked to him there . . .'

Rowan let this pass with a shrug. After a moment she said:
'And when will you be back?'

'Tomorrow, after we've finished our discussions.'

'That is unless you decide to stay on longer, I suppose – as
you did the other day.'

With patience heavy in his voice he said, 'Rowan, try to
understand. I don't punch a time clock, and on occasion –
very rarely – it's necessary for me to do things that might
possibly upset your plans – much as I hate to do it. I *know*
Alison and Geoff are coming round, and I know you've taken
great care in planning a really nice evening. But there's nothing I can do about it. I can't stay for it. I have to go. It's part
of my work.'

'All of a sudden you're interested in your work. That's a
novelty.'

She glared at him and he lowered his eyes under her gaze,
turned and went back into the house.

By six o'clock his briefcase and overnight bag were packed and
he was ready to leave. He couldn't go yet, though; not with
things as they were with Rowan. After hovering purposelessly
in the sitting room for a few minutes he went into the kitchen
where he found her busy at the stove. Much aware of stating
the obvious, he said: 'No word from Alison yet . . .'

'Not likely to be, either. Now Miss Carroll's phone is out of
order.'

'Are you sure?'

'I tried to call a couple of minutes ago – twice. Then I
checked with the operator. It's out of order.' She shook her
head distractedly. 'Here I am doing all this food and I don't even
know whether anybody's going to be here to eat the damned
stuff. I don't know *what* the hell's happening.' She picked up
the oven cloth, threw it down again and moved away across
the floor. 'I'd better get ready, anyway, just in case somebody
should come.'

He felt helpless and very conscious of the feeling that he
was leaving her in the lurch. 'Listen,' he said as he followed her

through the dining room, 'I'll drive over and see Alison. Find
out what's happening.'

'I thought you wanted to get off.'

'I don't need to go just yet. Besides, I'd like to see her before
I go – and say hello to Geoff . . . wish them good luck.'

They had reached the hall. At the foot of the stairs she
stopped and turned back to him. 'Well, you do what you want
to do, but it's up to Alison to let us know if she can't make it.
We shouldn't have to do the running around.'

'Well, with her phone out of order and Geoff only just
having got here she does have something of an excuse.
Anyway, they might not even be at The Laurels. Have you
called The Swan? They might be over there. I should think
that's most likely.'

'I already thought of that. She's not there, though. I phoned.
They told me that Mr Lucas checked in a while ago and then
went out again. They hadn't seen anything of Alison.'

'Look . . . I'll drive on over to The Laurels.'

She shrugged. 'Please yourself. But she was too busy to
come to the phone earlier and I'm not going to make the next
move. If they get here I shall be ready for them. If not – too
bad . . .' Turning away from him she started up the stairs.

At The Laurels Hal walked up the path and rang the bell.
There was some little delay before the door was opened but
then Miss Allardice was there, smiling up at him enquiringly.
He would, he said, if possible, like to see Mrs Lucas. Miss
Allardice gave a concerned, worried-looking little frown and
said: 'Oh, dear, I'm terribly sorry, but I'm afraid she's unable to
see anyone right now.'

Somewhat taken aback he hesitated for a moment then
said, 'But – well – could you please tell her that Hal Graham is
here . . . ? I think she'll see *me* . . .'

'I'm sorry.' Miss Allardice looked rather distressed. 'She
can't see anyone at all. Not anyone. She's – she's resting.'
Adding her sympathetic smile she started to close the door.

'Wait a minute –' Hal stepped forward. 'Please – uh – my

wife and I are wondering whether Mr and Mrs Lucas are coming round for dinner. We haven't heard anything from them . . .'

'I know nothing about that, I'm afraid.' She looked wide-
eyed into his face.

'I don't get it,' he said. He felt completely at a loss. 'I can't
believe she won't even *see* me – talk to me for a minute.'

She shrugged. 'I'm sorry, Mr Graham, but what can I say?
I'm only doing as I'm instructed.' She paused, then, lowering
her voice, added, 'You see – Miss Carroll is not at all well – and
Mrs Lucas is looking after her.'

'Oh . . .' He nodded, still not understanding.

'Miss Carroll, I'm afraid, is really very poorly,' Miss Allardice said. 'Poor Mrs Lucas – she's been up all night and most of
the day. As I say: now she's resting, but as soon as I can I'll tell
her you called. No doubt she'll be in touch with you.'

'Your phone's out of order,' he said. 'Did you know?'

'Oh, dear . . .' she clicked her tongue, 'if it isn't one thing it's
another.' With a final little smile and a nod she closed the door.

22

The tampon she discarded was barely stained. Her period was
over. A bare three days it had lasted; her usual time. She was
back to her regular pattern. All that hope, that promise; it had
all gone, leaving no sign now that there had ever been cause
for it to be.

Mechanically she showered, dried herself, got dressed and
began to brush her hair. After a while she heard the car pull
into the drive. Then Hal's feet sounded on the landing and he
came into the room. She looked at him in the glass as he stood
behind her. 'What did she say?' she asked.

'I didn't see her. According to Miss Allardice Alison's resting. She's been up all night looking after the old lady. Miss Carroll, apparently, is not at all well . . .'

Rowan was silent for a moment, then she said impatiently,
'Well, are they coming or not?'

He gave an infuriating shrug. 'Your guess is as good as mine.' Then he added, 'Offhand I'd say don't count on it. I'd say it's very doubtful.'

'But – she can't just leave it like *this*. She can't just – say nothing, do nothing . . . Did you ask to see her?'

'Of course I did. But Miss Allardice said she had instructions not to disturb her. No doubt Alison will be in touch, she said. Her words.'

Rowan got up and turned to him, shaking her head. 'This is *ridiculous*,' she said vehemently. 'The whole thing. She hasn't sent any message round; there's not been so much as a single word from her at all. It's suddenly as though we don't even *exist* for her.'

'So it seems.'

'But I don't understand it. There's got to be some explanation. For her to be so – uncaring and so – so cavalier . . . It's just not *like* her. Somehow it's all *wrong*.'

'I agree,' he said. He paused. 'But what's new? Every bloody thing seems wrong to me in this place.'

'*Please!*' She flapped her hands before him and then put them up to her ears. 'Not that. Please don't start on that again!'

He looked at her for a moment longer, then turned and went from the room.

A few minutes later when she went downstairs she found him in the sitting room, looking out onto the lawn.

'I thought you had somewhere to go,' she said.

He turned to her with his back to the window. 'What are you going to do?'

She shrugged. 'I don't know.' Then, knowing it would hurt, she added: 'Do you care that much?'

' – Rowan . . . don't.' He paused. 'Look – why don't you come with me? We'll spend two or three days in London.'

'You know I wouldn't like that. Why should I want to go there? I like it here. And anyway, what if Alison and Geoff turn up? Then what happens?'

'They're not coming now. You must realize that.'

'Oh, you're so sure about everything, aren't you? And if

you're that concerned about leaving me here, then don't go. Stay.'

'You know I can't do that. I've made all the arrangements. I've got to go.'

'You could phone him – that man, Goldman. See him another time. Or if he's that desperate to see you then let him come down here.'

'Aw, come on, Rowan, be sensible. I couldn't do that. And I can't change everything now. Look – this meeting is important.'

'It must be: you jumped at it fast enough.'

He sighed. 'This isn't getting us anywhere.'

'No, you're right, it isn't. You'd better get going or you won't get there tonight.'

He looked at her levelly for a second then started towards the door. As he went by her she added:

'And it's quite obvious that you can't wait to get away.'

He stopped, turned back to face her.

'You're right,' he said with quiet intensity, 'I *can't*.'

'So you admit it finally. It isn't just a case of your not settling, is it? You just don't like it here.'

He shook his head. 'No, I don't. I don't like it here, Rowan. I *hate* it here. I *hate* it. I *hate* this place. And the sooner we get away from it the better it'll be – for both of us!'

His hands were shaking, she could see; and there was anger in his eyes. 'Don't speak for me too,' she said.

'I *am*. I'm speaking for both of us. I know what I'm talking about.'

'Do you? You never ever gave the place a chance.'

'I've given it as much chance as I'm prepared to give. And I don't feel like giving it any more.' He paused. 'It's been at the back of my mind for days and days now – growing stronger all the time. And today I finally realized I'd had enough. As I came back from trying to see Alison I suddenly knew that that was it. It was just one more thing. Rowan – I've had this fucking village up to my eyeballs.'

'And now you're ready to pack up, are you? Just like that. Pack up and get out.'

'Oh, God . . .' He shook his head despairingly. 'This isn't the way I wanted to say it. Not like this. But, yes – that's what I want. And that's what I intend to do.'

'And what about me? I could have been happy here. I still could. I like this place.'

'We'll find somewhere else. Moorstone doesn't have a monopoly on old, characterful houses and pretty views. We'll find somewhere closer to London – as we originally planned. Some place that's not so completely cut off from everything we knew. Some place where we can still maintain some contact with the outside world.' His voice softened slightly. 'I know what it meant to you, coming here. You saw it all as some kind of – retreat – some kind of sanctuary. And I went along with it. I felt I had to. But it's not right for us. Maybe some other little village is, but not this one. This place – it's just not *real*. I don't know how to explain it but . . .' His words tailed off and he stepped towards her. 'Listen – don't think I've forgotten what it was like for you after Adam died, but – '

'Don't,' she cut in quickly. 'Don't. Don't bring him into it.'

'You see?' he said. 'You won't face anything. And you've got to. After Adam died I could understand you being desperate to get away. I could. But we can't do it forever. You can't deal with all your problems by just – cutting yourself off from them. At some time or other you've got to face up to them.'

'I thought I was doing that.'

'No, you're *not*. Somehow your – your colossal relief at getting away from the city and all those bad associations just – blinds you to everything else. This place – it *isn't* the answer to your prayers – our prayers. It's not the Garden of Eden. You might think it is, but it's not. There's something – wrong about this place, and I can't help but be aware of it.'

'Of what?' She could hear the scorn in her voice. 'Just what are you so aware of?'

'I don't know what it is. But there's some – undercurrent here. I can't explain it. But I feel it.' He moved closer to her. 'Rowan – I'm uneasy here.'

'But – *why*? For what reason? How can you be?'

He paused. 'Things – people – they just don't add up properly as they should. Things are not right. There are too many coincidences that are just – odd. I don't know any more than that. I just feel – I'm certain – that there's something going on in this place. I don't know what it is – and I don't intend staying around to find out.'

'So what *do* you intend doing?'

'I'm sorry to put it like this, but – well – when I've seen Goldman tomorrow I'm going to find a flat or something for us in London –'

'*No.*'

'Just a temporary place – where we can stay while we look around for something else. Someplace that will be good for us.'

' – But – this house. We haven't been here five minutes!'

'I can't help that. We'll sell it.'

'You've been making all these plans – for both of us.'

'Please – Rowan – I'm doing what I think is best.'

'Yes, *you're* doing it. And if I don't see it as the best thing for me?'

He stared at her. The only sound was the ticking of the clock. He shrugged. 'Then I would go on my own,' he said quietly.

For a few seconds neither spoke. Rowan turned and stood looking down the drive to where the car was parked. Hal stepped up behind her and put his hands on her shoulders.

'Look, I've got to go now,' he said. 'Why don't you turn off the oven, throw a few things into a case and come with me. I don't want to leave you like this. Come with me; we'll have a chance to talk.'

She shrugged his hands away. 'I don't think there's much left to say.' She gestured towards the car. 'Why don't you go before you leave it too late.'

She was still standing there in the same spot when she saw him get into the car and drive away.

She remained there for some moments after the car had gone

from sight, then went into the kitchen where she checked on the contents of the oven. He would be back soon, she was certain; he wouldn't *really* go off leaving the situation as it was between them. Taking a bottle of sherry she opened it, poured herself a glass and sat drinking it at the kitchen table. When the glass was empty she refilled it. After half an hour a third of the bottle's contents was gone and Hal had still not returned.

There never had been a situation like this before in their marriage, she reflected, and over the deep disappointment and hurt that had been with her over the past three days she felt anger, a sense of suffered injustice and betrayal. Mostly it was due to Hal, but Alison also played her part in it. By rights and by design, Rowan thought, she and Hal should have been welcoming Alison and Geoff for a pleasant evening together. Instead of which she was sitting here alone.

The aloneness was what she wanted, needed, least of all. She had to see someone, be with someone – and Alison was the only one right now who could help. She finished the glass of sherry that stood before her, got up, switched off the oven and left the house.

There were not many people abroad in the High Street, and of those who were most looked to be dressed in their Sunday clothes. She felt them staring curiously at her as she hurried by. She went to The Laurels, rang the bell and waited, breathless and distraught. After a few seconds Miss Allardice opened the door.

'Yes?' Her smile was very bright.

'Is Alison in?' Rowan asked.

'Yes, she is, but –'

Rowan cut in: 'I must see her. It's very important. Please tell her that I must see her.'

'Oh, dear, I'm so sorry.' Miss Allardice shook her head. 'She's not seeing *anyone* right now, I'm afraid.'

'But – but – please – at least tell her I'm here.' Rowan felt she was on the verge of tears. 'Please . . .'

Miss Allardice hesitated for a moment and then nodded. 'Just a minute.'

Rowan, left standing on the doorstep, watched as the other woman walked away along the hall and entered a door at the far end. Once Alison knew that it was she, Rowan, who wanted to see her she would agree at once, Rowan knew. The murmur of voices came drifting through the hall; women's voices; a man's voice was there too. Geoff's? It must be. Then there came a brief ripple of laughter, quickly dying.

Miss Allardice returned then, her head on one side and her face giving a look of sympathy. 'Just as I said, Mrs Graham. Mrs Lucas is terribly sorry but she can't see anyone right now.'

Rowan stared at her. 'But – did you tell her it was me . . . ?'

'Oh, yes, of course. I'm afraid she's frantically busy right now – with Miss Carroll. As I told your husband, Miss Carroll is very ill, and Mrs Lucas is caring for her. She asked me to tell you, though, that she'll be in touch with you tomorrow, without fail. In the meantime she sends you her apologies . . .'

The words were impossible for Rowan to accept. As Miss Allardice reached for the door Rowan said hurriedly, 'Well – Mr Lucas. Would you tell him that I'd like to see *him* for a moment, please?' Although she'd never met Geoff she knew that once she'd talked to him he would persuade Alison to see her. Miss Allardice just frowned, though, and said, 'Mr Lucas? He's not here.'

'He's not?'

'No. Oh, no. He was here earlier today but not now. I *believe* he's at The Swan.'

There was a moment of silence while Rowan hovered there, and then Miss Allardice, her sympathetic smile still in evidence, gently but firmly closed the door.

23

Hal had parked the car and was standing in line for his train ticket when he came to the decision not to go on. All the way to Exeter the doubts had been with him: should he turn back? should he continue on? Now, with the moment of commitment immediately before him he hesitated for just a moment longer and then stepped out of the queue.

In a nearby telephone kiosk he dialled the number of Crispin's House. He would tell Rowan that he was returning. There was no answer, though. After standing for some seconds with the ringing tone sounding monotonously in his ear he replaced the receiver and dialled Tim Farson's home number. Luckily the agent was in. Something had come up, Hal told him, and he couldn't get to London after all. Farson, clearly disappointed, said he supposed it couldn't be helped and that he'd pass on Hal's message and apologies to Goldman and try to fix another meeting soon.

That done, Hal left the station, got into the car and drove away.

Although he was returning to Moorstone he was going back on nothing he had said. He'd meant it all. He wasn't returning for good. They *would* leave that place – and the sooner the better. He would persuade Rowan that it was the best, the only, course for them; but he would do it reasonably, tactfully – not in the clumsy, brutal way he had already used. He realized now that he had allowed his unhappiness and doubt to come between them – just as Rowan's contentment in the place had, in turn, erected its own barriers. Whichever way you looked at it, it was Moorstone that had been the damaging factor.

Not, he reflected, that Rowan had seemed very content over the past few days. On the contrary, now that he thought back she had appeared despondent and very unhappy. Her unhappiness had not been due to her surroundings, though; that much was certain; she'd made that clear enough. With what, then? With *him*? No. He brushed the thought aside. They would get it all sorted out, very soon, and soon everything would be all right again.

One great mistake he had made, he realized, was in not confiding in her with regard to his doubts and the endless questions that had gradually formed in his mind over the weeks. Knowing how much the new environment had meant to her he had kept it all to himself – only giving intimation of his uneasiness to Alison – who shared his misgivings. And throughout it all he had been hoping, trusting, that the questions would be resolved and go away. But they had not. They had grown stronger and more numerous. In protecting Rowan he had built for them both a situation that had now become intolerable.

Now, though, he would tell her and at least *try* to convey to her some of the reasons for his own disquiet. He had spoken to her of an undercurrent in the place, of odd coincidences and the feeling that something was going on. Things were not right, he had said. And the more he thought about it all the more certain he was that it was so.

Crispin's House was empty when he got there.

The dining table was just as he had last seen it – set for three. The napkins lay folded just so, the glass and the silver gleaming. In the kitchen he found the oven turned off and the half-prepared food just left. On the table was an empty tumbler next to a part-empty bottle of sherry.

He went outside and checked in the garage. Her bicycle was still there. In the house again he dialled Alison's number. If she could be persuaded to leave Miss Carroll's sickbed for a moment perhaps she could tell him where Rowan was. He got the *number unobtainable* signal. It must still be out of order.

Lighting a cigarette he poured himself a drink, sat in his armchair in the sitting room and settled down to wait.

24

Rowan's shadow was long and black on the dark floor of the rock. Behind her the sun had lost most of its brilliance and was slowly sinking towards the horizon. From the east clouds were moving. A chill wind had sprung up. She sat in the centre of the wide, flat space, looking out over the village. As far as she could see the view spoke to her of nothing but peace and tranquillity – such things she so desperately needed for herself.

Following Alison's rebuff she had come up here to the Stone. She felt bewildered, and totally alone. Hal . . . and now Alison. And on top of the crushing disappointment over the Child. For that was how she had thought of it. But it never had been, she told herself; it had never even been the beginning. She had merely been a week late; it had been nothing more than a minor malfunctioning of her body.

Near her right foot was a dark stain just discernible in the fading light. There were splinters of glass there too. She could make out dusty footprints as well, scores of them, all over the floor of the rock. There had been many people up here, and recently. After a few more moments she got up and moved towards the rough-hewn steps. Into her mind came the memory of Alison's words when they had visited the Stone together: *I'll be bloody glad to get off this heap of rock. For some reason it gives me the creeps.* Touched briefly with the same cold feeling, Rowan quickly descended the steps and hurried away down the hillside.

She half walked, half ran along School Lane until she reached the High Street. Reaching it she paused for breath and in doing so caught a glimpse of her reflection in a shop window. Her hair was all awry. Her blue woollen dress was marked with dust from the Stone. Her hands were filthy and there was a dark smudge on her cheek. She turned away from the sight.

As she hurried on along the street she suddenly saw David Lockyer emerge from the main door of The Swan and cross over the road towards his front gate. He was right in front of her. Momentarily she checked her stride, coming to a halt. She felt she wanted to hide; she didn't want to see him; she didn't want to see anyone. It was pointless, though; he had seen her; there was nothing for it but to go on.

He was standing there at the gate as she drew level with him and she saw the look of surprise come over his face.

'Rowan . . .' He moved a step closer to her as she came to a hesitant stop on the pavement. 'What's the matter?' he asked. 'What's wrong?'

She just stood there, wordless. She knew that if she spoke she would cry. He spoke again, concern clear in his voice and his face:

'There's something wrong. What is it? Tell me.'

Briefly closing her eyes she shook her head and made to step past him. He reached out, though, and grasped her firmly but gently by the arm. He turned her towards him and looked into her face.

'What's happened?' he said. 'Please, tell me . . .'

She made no answer.

'Where are you hurrying off to like this? Home?'

Another shake of the head in reply: no; she didn't know . . .

'I think you'd better come in for a minute,' he said.

He opened the gate and she allowed him to lead her along the path to the front door and into the house. In the cluttered sitting room she sat on the sofa. He took an armchair facing her.

'Something's very wrong, isn't it?' he said.

The gentleness and the compassion she heard in his voice were all that were needed to break down the last of her self-control. Putting her hands up to her face she began to cry.

Lockyer, she became aware, was now at her side, one large hand on her shaking shoulder. He said nothing; just let her weep, waiting for her sobbing to cease. After some minutes she grew quiet again and she took the Kleenex he held ready and wiped her eyes and blew her nose.

'I'm sorry,' she said, sniffing, 'the only time I ever seem to see you is when I'm in some kind of trouble.'

As she turned to look at him he gave a smile. 'Anytime,' he said, 'if I can be of help.'

She nodded her thanks.

'Would you like to tell me what kind of trouble you're in now?' he asked.

'Oh . . .' She felt the tears might return and she took a deep breath and fought to control herself. 'I – I don't know,' she said hoarsely after a moment. 'I just – just feel that – everything's gone wrong. Everything.'

'What has gone wrong?'

She shook her head. She couldn't tell him about the baby, about Hal, about Alison. . . . 'Just – everything,' she repeated.

He looked at her for a few seconds then got up. 'I think I'll have a drink,' he said. 'I've just had a couple in The Swan, but now I think I could do with another. I think you could as well.'

She said nothing.

'Is whisky okay?' he said.

'Fine.' She whispered it.

He poured the drinks, handed her one and sat beside her again. 'We seem to have done all this before,' he said.

'Don't remind me.' She was aware of his closeness.

'Is your hand all right now?'

'Yes, thank you.'

'And have you settled in all right? You've had a few weeks here now.'

After a moment's hesitation she said: 'We're leaving.'

'Leaving? You're going away from here – from Moorstone?'

'Yes.'

'But why?'

'It's not *my* decision.'

'Your husband?'

'Yes. He's set on it now. He doesn't like it here. He can't settle.'

'That's a pity . . .'

'Yes . . . it is.' Sadly she shook her head. 'And I was just beginning to feel I belonged here, too.' Suddenly she got up. 'Oh, God, just listen to me! I just come here and pour out all my troubles to you. It's unforgivable.' Turning, she caught sight of her reflection in the glass above the fireplace. She'd quite forgotten what a spectacle she made. 'And *look* at me! It's enough to frighten anyone to death.' Making an effort to smile she said: 'Would you mind if I washed my face and put a comb through my hair?'

In the bathroom she washed her face and hands and used

his comb to put her hair in order. Afterwards in his small hall-
way she brushed some of the marks from her dress. When she
returned to the sitting room he held out her glass to her. She
saw that it had been refilled. 'You look a little different now,' he
said, smiling.

'Well, that's something.' She took a sip from the glass and
sat down again. 'When I've finished this I must go,' she said.
She was still feeling the effects of the sherry.

They talked as they sat in the quiet, comfortable room,
but the talk didn't always come easily and it was interspersed
with silences. She was so aware of being there with him, in his
house, alone. At last she put down her empty glass and rose
from her seat. 'I really must go,' she said. 'Leave you in peace.'

'Please – don't go on my account. I don't have anything special to do.'

She shrugged. 'Anyway, I . . .' Her words tailed off. Then she
said, 'Could I – do you mind if I use your phone?'

'Of course not.'

She moved to the telephone, dialled, listened for a while
and then replaced the receiver. So he hadn't come back. He
had gone on to London.

'Nobody home?' Lockyer said.

'Nobody home.'

'Was it important?'

'No.' She shook her head. Taking a couple of steps towards
the door she added, 'Anyway . . . I'd better go . . .'

'I'll drive you home.'

'No . . . no . . .' She paused. 'I'm not going home. Not yet.'

'Isn't he expecting you? Hal?'

'He's in London.'

Lockyer had got up from the sofa and now stood just a
couple of feet away from her. They faced one another.

'Why don't you stay a while longer?' he said gently, smiling.

She looked at him for another moment then lowered her
eyes and turned away. She shrugged. 'Why not?'

It wasn't right. No part of it was working out the way it was supposed to. Lockyer was moving within her and all she could do was ask herself the question *What am I doing here?* She had expected, *hoped*, to derive some kind of comfort from all this. But there was none. There was no warmth. There was no pleasure. There was nothing. There was just this man who was slamming into her body. This man who, in filling her, only added to her emptiness; his every stroke only serving to tear aside the flimsy curtain that had disguised the reality behind it, only driving deeper within her her growing despair.

When it was all over and he lay panting at her side she lay stone-cold sober and unmoving, staring with dull eyes up at the ceiling.

25

It was almost ten o'clock. Hal had just dialled the number of The Swan and asked to speak to Mrs Lucas. After a short wait he heard a man's voice on the line.

'Yes?'

'May I speak to Mrs Lucas, please?'

'She's not here.'

'Oh . . .' Hal paused. ' – Is that Mr Lucas? – Geoff?'

'Yes, who's this?'

'My name's Hal Graham. I'm a friend of Alison's.'

'Ah, yes – she wrote to me about you and your wife.' The voice sounded weary.

'Do you expect Alison back soon?'

'No, I don't. Have you tried The Laurels? – Miss Carroll's place?'

'She's still there?'

'I would imagine so.'

Hal thanked him and hung up. How strange, he thought, that Lucas should be at the hotel alone. After a moment he dialled The Laurels again. Still no ringing tone. He went outside, got onto his bicycle and rode away from the house.

For the second time that day he found himself striding up the front path of The Laurels and ringing the bell. Once again the door was opened by Miss Allardice. She looked rather surprised to see him and gave a swift, pointed glance at her watch. Then, with a smile, she said, 'Mr Graham – and what can we do for you *this* time?'

'I'm sorry to trouble you again,' he said, ' – and at such a late hour, but I wonder – is it possible for me to see Mrs Lucas now? It's most important.' As she hesitated, frowning, he added insistently, '*Please . . .*'

She gave a reluctant nod. 'I'll go and see if she's about. Would you wait . . . ?' Turning, she moved back through the hall. After a minute or two she had returned. 'Yes,' she said, 'she can see you now.'

He stepped over the threshold and followed her towards the drawing room. Reaching the door, Miss Allardice gestured for him to go in, then turned and went away.

As he entered he saw Alison get up from a chair. She came towards him, smiling rather ruefully.

'Hal,' she said, 'how can you and Rowan ever want to talk to me again after letting you down so badly? I *am* sorry. Can you ever forgive me?'

He waved a dismissing hand. 'Well, we were disappointed, of course, but mostly, I think, rather puzzled. It just didn't – seem like you.'

'I'm sure it didn't. I'm sorry. Truly. Here, come and sit down for a moment.' She waved him towards the sofa. He shook his head.

'No, I can't stay. I only came here to ask whether you've seen anything of Rowan . . .'

'She was here earlier. Though I didn't see her. I was asleep. God, I was so tired. I was on my feet all night.' She paused. 'Why, what's up? Has something happened? Don't you know where she is?'

'No. I'm afraid we had a bit of bust-up. She went out somewhere and hasn't come back. I'm beginning to get rather – concerned.' He shrugged. 'I was hoping she was with you. When was it she called here, do you know?'

'Oh, about seven, I believe.'

Wearily he nodded. He felt at a loss. He took out his cigarettes, offered her one. She shook her head. 'No, thank you. I'm giving it up.' Frowning, she added: 'You'd better not smoke in here, Hal. – Miss Carroll would be most – displeased.'

'Oh, yes . . . sorry.' He put the cigarettes back in his pocket. 'I'm told that Miss Carroll's not at all well,' he said.

'No, I'm afraid not. Paul Cassen's just been to see her again. But there's nothing he can do for her, it seems.'

'What's the problem?'

She hesitated for a second then said quietly: 'She's just . . . well, I'm afraid she's just – gone quite mad.'

' – She's *insane*?'

'Absolutely. It's terrible. We've had to restrain her.' Here she pulled up the sleeve of her blouse to reveal several bruises and long, deep scratches. 'Thank God Miss Allardice was here,' she said. 'I don't know what I'd have done otherwise. I couldn't have held her on my own.'

'It's as bad as *that*!' Hal looked aghast. 'I had no idea.'

'No, why should you have? It came as a complete shock to me, too. But perhaps now you can understand why I seemed so – ' She shrugged. 'Well, let's just say I've had a few difficulties to cope with.'

'And how is she now?'

'No better. We've had to shut her in her room. I don't know – she seems to be suffering from the strangest delusions or something. I don't understand these things.'

'So what's going to happen?'

'They're sending an ambulance for her. Paul says it's the only thing to do. They'll take her to Primrose House.' She shook her head. 'It's awful, I know. But what else can we do? She can't be cared for here.' Touching her bruised arm she added wonderingly, 'Who would have dreamed that such an old lady would have so much strength?'

'When I saw her the other day she seemed so rational and so – well balanced.'

'I know. It's all so sad.'

After a moment he said sympathetically, 'And all this has come at the worst possible time for you, hasn't it? What with Geoff returning and everything . . .'

'Yes . . .' She paused. 'But that's another matter altogether.' She turned away from him and crossed over to the window.

'I talked to him on the phone not long ago,' he said. 'He told me he wasn't expecting you at the hotel . . .'

'No.' She kept her back to him. 'I'm afraid things have changed between Geoff and me. It's all over between us.'

He didn't understand her. She couldn't be serious. Was this the girl who'd been counting the hours to her husband's return?

After a moment she said sadly: 'When a person's been away for any length of time one tends to forget what they're really like. You only remember the good things – and even those your memory makes seem better than they actually were.' She turned back to face him. 'It's so sad how things work out sometimes, isn't it?'

'Do you mean that? It really is finished between you?'

'Yes.'

'So you won't be going away with him now . . .'

'No.'

'So what will you do? Go back to Brighton?'

'No. I think I shall stay on here for a while.'

'In Moorstone?'

'Why not?'

'But – but the way you've talked about it before . . . You couldn't wait to get away.'

'Ah . . .' She smiled and gave a shrug. 'I probably said quite a few rather foolish things. Still, that's in the past. They do say that a lady's entitled to change her mind.'

'Where will you stay in the village? What will you do?'

'I'll stay *here* – in this house. Where else? Believe me, there's no shortage of work to be done. Besides – who knows? – Miss Carroll might recover. It's extremely doubtful that she will, but *if* she does then she'll need me. No, this is much the best place for me to be.'

As she finished speaking the door opened and a man entered. Hal recognized the librarian, Ralph Collins.

'Oh, I'm sorry,' Collins said, 'I didn't realize you had company.'

'That's all right. You know Mr Graham, don't you?'

'Of course. How do you do?'

Hal returned the greeting and then said, 'Well, I'd better go.' He moved away in the direction of the hall. Turning in the doorway he said, 'Please – if Rowan should come back – well – ask her to come on home, will you?'

'Of course.' Alison had followed him. 'But don't worry about her. She'll probably be there by the time you get back.'

'Yes, I expect so . . .'

'And Hal – just let me see an end to my present difficulties and we'll get together for that dinner.'

'Oh, right . . . fine . . .' He gave a nod then added, 'It's all right, I'll see myself out.'

He wished her and Collins goodbye, went into the hall and towards the front door. As he opened it he saw a vehicle with bright headlights pull up at the gate. The ambulance, come to take Miss Carroll away. Turning, he stepped back to the drawing room where the door had been left partly open. About to say, 'The ambulance is here,' he reached out to open the door wider – and then came to an abrupt halt. Through the aperture he saw them. Collins and Alison. He had his arm around her, one hand upon her breast. She was smothering his face with kisses.

Quickly, silently, Hal turned and moved away.

Two white-coated young men were getting out of the ambulance as he approached the gate. They nodded to him as they went past him towards the house. As he got astride his bicycle he looked back and saw Miss Allardice opening the door to them. The next moment they'd gone inside.

Suddenly his eyes were drawn to an upper window. A light there had blinked on and off. And as he looked the light came on again, and stayed. And then he saw there the figure of Miss Carroll. She was gesticulating – to *him* – her hands waving frantically, bidding him to go to her. Even from where he stood he could see the look of wildness about her, the dishevelment of her hair and clothing.

He stayed there for a moment longer and then, shocked and saddened, turned from the sight and rode away.

As he approached Crispin's House his bicycle lamp shone on a large car drawn up in the drive. He stopped beside it and a tall man got out and came towards him. Hal tensed at the sight of the unknown, shadowy figure. 'Yes?' he said. 'Can I help you?'

'Are you Mr Graham . . . ?'

The voice sounded vaguely familiar. 'Yes, I am,' Hal said, peering at him.

'I'm Geoffrey Lucas.'

'Ah . . . yes . . .' Hal relaxed. 'Hello.'

'Hello . . .' There was a brief pause, then Lucas added, 'I know it's late but – could I see you for a minute?'

'Of course.' Hal leant the bicycle against the garage wall. 'Come on in.'

There was no sign of life in the house. Obviously Rowan was still out. Hal turned on the lights and led the way into the sitting room. 'Sit down,' he said. 'Can I get you a drink?'

'No, thanks.' Lucas sat on the sofa. He was slimly built; his hair was very fair, his fine, strong features suntanned. Hal placed his age at about forty.

'I hope you don't mind me calling on you like this,' Lucas said. 'I just had to talk to someone.' He paused and shook his head. 'I arrive in this place and Alison is – God, I don't know. I just don't know what the hell is going on.'

'I don't think I can be of any help to you,' Hal said. 'I'm as much in the dark as you are.'

'Have you seen her?'

'Yes. I've just come back from The Laurels now.'

'And you actually did see her?'

'Yes, just briefly.'

'Did she mention me?'

'Well – yes . . .'

A pause. 'What did she say? Tell me – please . . .'

Hal shrugged. Awkwardly he said, 'She said something about – about things having changed between you . . .'

Lucas nodded. Bitterly he said, 'Christ, I'll say they have. Though not on my side. She's the one who's changed. So much. I still can't believe it. Her letters – right up to the time I left – they gave no indication whatsoever that I should be prepared for anything like this. On the phone, too. I talked to her on the phone just a couple of days ago, and she seemed so excited over the fact that I was coming back.' He shook his head. 'And then I get back and find her like this. I'd never have thought it possible. She won't even talk to me – not now. We just had the one meeting – at The Laurels this afternoon. And that was it. It's over, she told me. Just like that. It's over.'

Silence fell in the room. Hal could think of nothing to say. After a few moments Lucas went on: 'I don't know what to do. I'll stay at the hotel for tonight and try to get to see her again tomorrow. If she won't, well . . .' he shrugged, sighed, '. . . I'll just – pack up and go.'

'Perhaps – perhaps things might work out – if you hang on for a while longer,' Hal said, not believing his own words. He felt helpless. 'I mean – what with her employer – Miss Carroll – being taken ill like that – perhaps Alison's suddenly under too much of a strain.'

'No . . . I'd like to think that might be it, but I know it's not. Her whole attitude towards me is different. Her whole manner. She's just not the same. She's going to stay on here in the village, she told me. She's quite determined. All our plans – our love for each other – it's as if none of it ever existed.' Briefly his eyes closed in anguish. 'I just can't get over how she was with me. So cold, so distant. She treated me as if I were a stranger.' His voice broke on the last word and Hal watched uncomfortably as tears sprang into his eyes. After a little while, and with a visible effort to control himself, Lucas went on: 'She told me she's got work to do here. She said she's going to finish writing Miss Carroll's book.' He shook his head. 'She's never had the slightest inclination to write anything in the past. But there's more to it than that. There's also that fellow there – Collins, I think his name is.'

With Lucas's words Hal relived the moment, not long before, when he had seen Alison wrapped in Collins's arms. Then Lucas was speaking again.

'He was there when I went to the house,' he said. 'And I could tell at once that there was something between them – even before she mentioned it. You could see the way they were with one another. It was so clear. And then she told me. She was in love with him, she said.' He gazed keenly at Hal. 'Were *you* aware of it – before? Did you know about them? – her and that fellow Collins?'

' – No, I didn't . . .' All Hal knew of any feeling between Alison and Collins was that she had hated him . . .

Lucas was getting to his feet. Hal also arose. They stood facing one another.

'You're a complete stranger,' Lucas said, 'and I've just come here and – burdened you with my problems. I'm sorry. I suppose I just hoped that you might be able to – give me some hope – or at least some explanation – tell me something that would make it easier to understand. Going by her letters you and your wife were the only people she felt anything for . . .' He paused then asked, 'I don't suppose your wife would know anything that . . .'

'She doesn't know any more than I do,' Hal said quickly. 'And she's not in right now.' He shook his head sadly. 'I wish there was something I could do to help . . . There's nothing. Alison – she's – she's quite different with us as well.'

Lucas took his car keys from his pocket, stared unseeingly at them for a moment then said bitterly, 'Oh, Christ! How I wish to God she'd never come to this place.' Then he reached out, briefly grasped Hal's hand and turned quickly for the door.

When Lucas had gone Hal put his bicycle into the garage beside the car, turned off the downstairs lights and went up to his study. In his seat at his desk he sat smoking, waiting and watching for Rowan's return. From here he could see the road to the village. His anxiety was increasing by the moment. It was almost midnight now. He would wait a little while longer and then contact the police.

When his imagination wasn't running riot he thought of his visit to The Laurels and his subsequent encounter with Geoff Lucas. Who would have believed that Alison could change so dramatically – and in such a short time? She had turned her back on everything she had known before – her husband, her plans, her friendships – and now embraced what she'd previously regarded as anathema to her – living in the village, the attentions of Ralph Collins. In addition to that she had now declared her intention to *write* – something in which hitherto she'd shown not the slightest interest.

He thought of her earlier suspicious regard of the village, its inhabitants and the strange pattern of events that had become apparent. 'All those young people who come to Moorstone for a visit or something and end up staying, making it their home,' she had said. 'They all seem to, don't they?' And then she had added: 'But here's one who won't. When I leave on Monday with Geoff that will be it.'

But she was staying, and her husband was leaving Moorstone alone. Her suspicions now seemed not to exist. All that talk about Mary Hughes and Miss Larkin, Paul Cassen and Dr Richmond, David Lockyer and Edwin Leclerc; it meant nothing at all to her now.

For now she had become a part of that very same pattern. She was staying on in the village – and Miss Carroll had been taken to Primrose House.

Mary Hughes and Miss Larkin, Paul Cassen and Dr Richmond, David Lockyer and Edwin Leclerc – and now Alison and Edith Carroll. . . .

He took another cigarette from the packet before him. As he did so he saw, over to the west, a small pinpoint of light. Cigarette forgotten he switched off the lamp. Now, in the darkness, he could see better. Other lights were appearing. They were over on the distant hillside, close to the Stone.

26

When Rowan saw Crispin's House come in view a great feeling of relief swept over her. Although her earlier phone call had got no answer the present confirmation of Hal's absence was what she had prayed for. So afraid had she been of finding him there, waiting, she had scarcely dared to look. But it was all right; the windows were all dark.

As they approached the corner she said to Lockyer without looking at him, 'Pull up here, will you?' As he stopped the car she glanced at the clock on the dashboard. It was after midnight.

'Will you be all right?' Lockyer asked.

'Yes.' She didn't look at him. She couldn't. She just sat there, fingers clasping and unclasping.

'What's the matter?' he asked. When she didn't answer he said: 'It's a bit late for regrets, you know.'

'I know.'

'It's done. There's nothing we can do to change it.'

'I know that.'

Pressing down the handle she got out. Then, without answering his goodnight she slammed the door behind her and walked away. After a moment the car started up again, drove past her, made a U-turn at the corner of Crispin's Lane and then sped past her again, moving back towards the village. After it had gone by she stopped, turned and watched as its tail lights disappeared round the curve in the road. Then she turned once more and walked towards the house.

When she reached the gate she stood for a few seconds leaning on it. David Lockyer was right – it was no good spending time regretting what had happened. She would have given anything to undo the events of the past few hours but it was too late; they couldn't be undone. She could only thank God that Hal was away. At least by the time he returned tomorrow she would, hopefully, have begun to come to terms with it. She would have to, for he must never know.

She pushed open the gate. As she closed it she saw up on the distant hill a cluster of tiny lights, near to where the Stone rose up. Raising her head higher she looked up at the night sky. The stars were sharp and clear. It was a fine night. Hal would be at his club in London, sleeping. Tomorrow morning he would be meeting the film producer, Goldman. In the afternoon he'd be putting in motion those wheels that would eventually see their departure from Moorstone. She thought of David Lockyer again. She was ready to leave now. The sooner the better.

As she went into the house the thought uppermost in her mind was that she must shower. She must do that before she could even begin to think of sleeping. She hurried up the stairs.

She had almost reached the top when Hal stepped from his darkened study and stood before her.

She started so violently that she briefly missed her footing and had to clutch the banister for support. Heart thudding she stared up at him, suddenly cold, the sweat breaking out under her arms. 'Hal . . .' she said after too long a moment. She forced a smile that felt stiff on her lips. 'God, but you – you gave me a shock.'

He stood looking down at her. When he spoke his voice was very quiet. 'Where have you been?' he said.

She didn't answer. After a moment she lowered her eyes and turned her head away.

'Rowan,' he said, 'it's gone twelve. You've been out for hours. I've been worried sick.'

She remained silent. Turning to look at him again she saw that he was still staring at her, his brows furrowed.

'Say something,' he said. 'Don't just stand there.'

'I – I thought you'd gone to London,' she said at last.

'How *could* I go?' He paused. 'What have you been doing all this time? Where have you been?'

She shrugged. 'Just . . . walking . . .'

'*Walking? All this time?*'

She shook her head distractedly. 'I just – wanted to get away

– to think. Please, Hal – all these questions. Stop – cross-examining me. I'm tired. I want to go to bed.' She moved up the remaining stairs and he stepped back. When she was on the landing, though, he came forward again and stood in her path.

'I got back here and there was no sign of you,' he said. 'I've been looking for you everywhere. I went to see Alison . . . I was just about to call the police. Tell me – where have you been?'

'I *told* you,' she said sharply, a note of hysteria in her voice, 'I've been walking.'

'But what *else* have you been doing? Rowan, I just want to know. It's obvious to anyone that you couldn't have been walking all this time.'

'Oh, for God's sake, *stop*!' She was on the verge of tears now. She moved to step around him but he reached out and held her arm. With a quick, violent movement she wrenched herself free but as quickly he took hold of her again, this time with both hands. 'Why won't you tell me where you were?' he said reasonably, 'and with whom?'

' – I haven't been with anyone. I went to see Alison at The Laurels but – '

He broke in: 'That was much earlier. I know about that. She told me. I'm talking about afterwards.' Still with his hands on her shoulders he added, 'What I don't understand is why you should lie. Why are you lying to me, Rowan?'

'I'm *not lying* to you. For God's sake . . .' She couldn't meet his eyes as she spoke.

'If you're not lying to me then how was it you came home in David Lockyer's car?'

She could feel the shock register on her face. 'Ah, so you were spying on me,' she said. 'Sitting up here in the dark, waiting to catch me out.'

She knew the moment she had uttered the words that they were the worst she could have chosen. She knew it and she could see it reflected in his expression.

'No,' he said with a little shake of his head, 'I wasn't spying on you, Rowan. I was sitting looking at the lights up by the Stone. And then I saw the car pull up just down the road.

Just afterwards, when it turned at the corner, I recognized it. Lockyer's the only one in the village who drives a Jaguar.' He paused. 'No, I wasn't spying on you. Did I have reason to spy on you? To wait to catch you out?' Another pause. 'They were your words,' he added.

She could say nothing. She could feel the treacherous seconds going by, taking her further beyond the point at which some explanation might have saved her. Now, in just a brief time she knew that any words at all were useless.

It seemed to her that they stood without moving for a long time. And then she was aware of his hands moving slowly from her shoulders, sinking wearily to his sides. When at last he spoke his voice was little more than a whisper.

'You've been with him. Lockyer . . .'

She didn't answer. He must have been able to read the guilt in her face as clearly as if it were written there. There was another silence, then he said softly, his words sounding faintly pleading:

'Rowan . . . tell me that I'm – letting my imagination run away with me. Tell me – please.'

Still unable to answer she closed her eyes, and the tears that had threatened welled up and ran down her cheeks. It was all the answer he could want. When she looked up a few moments later he was turning, moving past her towards the stairs. She stood without moving for some minutes after he had gone and then hurried after him.

She reached the hall in time to see him emerge from the sitting room. They each came to a stop, looking at one another. He held his briefcase in one hand and his overnight case in the other. His raincoat was over his arm.

'I should have gone to London,' he said, 'as you so obviously thought I had.' He shook his head. 'Jesus Christ, Rowan, did you have to make such an idiot of me?' He moved to the door, hesitated for a moment then turned towards her once more.

'Anyway,' he said, 'I'm going up to London now. Exactly when I'll be back I can't say.'

'Let me come with you,' she said.

'No. I think I'd prefer to be on my own for a while. Besides, you had your chance earlier. You didn't want to then.' He reached out for the door handle.

'Hal – ' she said, then waited till he was facing her again. 'Hal, I – I love you . . .'

'Terrific,' he said, nodding. 'And you certainly have a way of showing it.'

The next moment he had opened the door and was stepping out into the dark. Minutes later there came the sound of the car starting up and moving down the drive and onto the road.

27

It was unusual to see the people of Moorstone about at such a late hour. Usually by this time of night the whole place was asleep. Tonight, though, for some reason, things were different. Approaching the bridge he noticed several figures moving before him down Little Street. Far ahead he could make out the shape of the Stone; see the tiny, winking lights moving around its base. Then he was turning away from the sight, moving left into the High Street. And there were people here too, all going in the same direction. As he went by he noticed that many of them paused to stare at the car. Let them stare if they had nothing better to do. Whatever they did was no longer any concern of his. He was not one of them. He never had been and he never would be. When he next set eyes on this place it would merely be for the purpose of selling the house and collecting his belongings. He would never ever come to live in Moorstone again.

But what of Rowan . . . ?

That was a question he couldn't even begin to answer. After what had happened tonight he was no longer sure of anything where Rowan was concerned.

★

He had driven about three miles out of the village when, rounding a curve, he suddenly saw the figure of a woman appear in the glare of his headlights. It was like history repeating itself . . . Not quite, though. Unlike Miss Larkin, this woman seemed intent on self-preservation, for in the moment that he turned the wheel to avoid her she became aware of the car's approach and dodged into the shadow of the hedgerow. He'd had time to recognize her, though. That small, slightly bent figure clad in shawl and long skirts – it could only be Miss Carroll.

But what was she doing out here so late in the night? After some hesitation he pulled over to the side, braked and waited for her to draw level. But she didn't, and when after some moments there was still no sight of her he switched off the motor, took the torch from the glove compartment and got out of the car.

A cold wind had sprung up. He stood still for a few moments and then began to walk back along the road, moving the light in a sweeping arc. There was no sign of her at all. He continued on. And then he saw her there – cowering against the hedgerow. As the torch beam fell on her face she gave a whimpering little cry, raised her arm across her eyes and pressed herself deeper into the shadows.

'Miss Carroll . . . ?'

She didn't move. He lowered the torch so that its glare fell on the grass at her feet. The moonlight was enough. 'It's all right,' he said. 'It's all right.'

Now at his words he watched her tense, and then lower her shielding arm. 'Who *is* that?' she said. 'You blinded me with that light.'

'I'm sorry.' He was about to give his name when she cut in, saying: 'It's Hal, isn't it? Hal Graham.'

'You recognized my voice.'

'Of course.' Then she added, 'And I can see you now.'

As he moved closer to her she stepped out of the shadow and stood before him. The wind was moving her hair and blowing her shawl against her body. She looked very small and frail.

'You shouldn't be out here,' he said. 'You'll get cold . . .'

She paused and then shrugged. 'I have to get away from that place.'

'The village?'

'Yes.'

'Look,' he said after a moment, 'why don't you come and sit in the car . . . ?'

She drew away from him. 'You want to take me back, don't you?'

'No, of course not.'

'You mean that?'

'Of course.'

She moved towards him again. 'Where are you going?' she asked.

'To London.'

'Now? You're going there now?'

'Yes.'

'Good.' She gave a nod of satisfaction. 'And you must never come back. Never.'

Seeing her before him now he remembered his last sight of her – only a few hours earlier – when she'd stood at the upper window of The Laurels. She didn't look nearly so wild now. He could make out no hint of madness in her eyes. He saw there only a kind of bewildered despair; a look that made him think once more of Miss Larkin – as she had stood on the edge of the chalkpit.

As if she'd been able to read some of his thoughts the woman said, 'I'm not mad, you know. Oh, I know they'd tell you I am, but I'm not.' She paused. 'Though what they've done would be enough to drive the strongest person insane.'

'What is that? What *have* they done?'

She stared at him for a moment as if deliberating, then slowly she shook her head. 'If I told you that, at this moment, you'd believe they were right.' She shivered and pulled the shawl more closely about her shoulders. The wind was growing stronger now and scudding clouds intermittently shut out the light from the moon. 'Primrose House,' she said. 'They took me to Primrose House.'

He nodded. 'I know.'

'Not for long, though. I got out again. I don't think they could have cared that much. Now, if I died of exposure or something – they'd be relieved. That would be one less to bother about.' She frowned. 'I got out quite easily. There was hardly anyone about.'

'I'm not surprised. They're all off somewhere for some purpose or other. The whole village.'

'What do you mean?'

'I don't know. There's something going on. Some kind of stupidity, I suppose. They're all heading towards the Stone, it looked like. Everyone's out on the streets.'

'*Now?* Tonight?'

'Yes. I saw them all as I came by. And there are lights up by the Stone.'

'Oh, Christ.' She stared at him for a moment then, stepping forward, pushed at him with one small hand. 'You must go,' she said. 'Go. Now. Don't just stand around here.'

'What for?'

'Just go.'

He didn't understand her. 'What about you?' he said.

'Would you – take me with you?'

'To London?'

She nodded.

'Yes,' he said, 'of course.'

Reaching out to him again she said, 'Then we must go quickly.' She took his arm and together they went to the car. As he opened the rear door for her she straightened and said, 'You're alone?'

'Yes . . .'

'But – where's Rowan?'

'She – she's at the house.'

Frantically she shook her head. 'You mustn't leave without her. You must get her.'

As she finished speaking she climbed into the car. He closed the door after her and got into the driver's seat. She leaned towards him. 'Turn it around,' she said, 'and hurry!'

He still didn't understand. But whether she was mad or not he couldn't ignore the urgency in her voice. He got the car moving and drove down the road looking for a suitable place in which to turn. Eventually he found a spot at the entrance to a field. As he reversed into the opening he was suddenly aware of the old woman leaning forward and taking his cigarettes from the seat beside him. He stopped the car and turned to face her.

'I need this,' she said.

He watched as she struck a match. When the flame had gone her face was all in shadow again. But he could feel her old eyes watching him above the glowing end of the cigarette. He stared at her as she sighed and blew out the smoke.

'What are you waiting for?' she said. 'We must hurry.'

He ignored her words. He should have realized earlier that there was something different about her. There had been so many signs.

'Miss – Miss Carroll . . . ?' he said.

He could make out the slow shake of her head.

'No, Hal,' she said. Her voice sounded resigned and utterly weary now. She put the matches into the seat pocket before her and leaned back. 'No, not Miss Carroll,' she said. 'Not *really* Miss Carroll.'

28

Standing under the shower Rowan washed the touch of David Lockyer from her body. Then, wrapping herself in a towel, she went next door into the bedroom, where she dried herself and put on her nightdress. She felt as though she were moving in a dream.

Sitting on the edge of the bed she looked dully at her reflection in the mirror. The sight of the long white gown with its intricate decoration of lace made her wonder why she'd bothered putting it on. She wasn't going to be able to sleep. She never wanted to sleep here again. The house and the village

– each had lost its magic for her. She got up, stepped into her slippers and pulled on her dressing gown.

She began to pace the room. Hal had gone. And there was no knowing when he would be back; if he ever did come back. But this last thought she tried to dismiss from her mind. He *would* come back. He had to. Maybe not for a while, but he would return in the end.

But then, she realized, she couldn't wait. It might be days before he came back, and she couldn't wait that long. . . .

Abruptly ceasing her pacing she got a suitcase from the cupboard, opened it up on the bed and began to pack it. Tomorrow, as soon as it was light, she would leave. She'd go to Exeter and get a train for London. She'd find him at his club. Everything would be all right then. It would have to be.

Behind her on the bed her suitcase lay packed and closed.

She sat at the window, looking out into the night.

The lights up by the Stone seemed to be growing in number. Something was happening up there. . . . She shivered and pulled her dressing gown more closely around her. Things were different tonight. She could sense something; something that was not – *right*. It was almost like the barely discernible vibration of some weird, unknowable undercurrent. It even pervaded the house. It was not due simply to her anxiety following Hal's departure; it was something more.

Mesmerized, she continued to stare at the lights. She seemed unable to keep her eyes from the sight. What was it that was happening up there?

As she sat there, so still, she suddenly realized that she had become aware of the beating of her own heart. Putting her hand to her breast she found that her palm was wet with perspiration. The realization that she was afraid brought with it its own measure of fear.

But what was she afraid of? With an attempt to brush her unnamed fears aside she urged herself to be calm. But it was no good; the fear persisted and grew stronger. And then into her mind came a picture of herself sitting alone and exposed at the window of the lighted room. Immediately she got up and reached for the curtain cord.

Even after the curtains were drawn she remained standing there, eyes wide, as if still looking down towards the end of the drive. And her fear had grown even more – for now there was something to which it could be attached.

In the moment before the curtains had come together she had caught a fleeting glimpse of two figures. They had been standing side by side in the shadows by the gate. Her view of them had lasted only an instant, nevertheless she was sure she had recognized them . . .

She backed away from the window. Mrs Palfrey and Tom Freeman . . . what were they doing – waiting there, watching the house . . . ?

29

He wouldn't take the risk of driving through the village so instead he took a roundabout route back towards Crispin's House, approaching it now from the north-east. Neither, he felt, was it safe to get too close with the car, so, coming to within a hundred yards of the gate he turned the car around and parked it in a dark, overhung spot where there was little chance of its being seen.

He switched off the engine and the lights and then turned quickly to the figure of the old woman who sat pressed into the corner of the seat behind him. Way back there on the lonely road she had given him the answers to so many of his questions. It had taken very little time. And there was little now that he needed to know.

'Will you be all right here?' he asked. She'd covered herself with his raincoat. All he could make of her face was a pale blur.

'Yes,' she said wearily. 'I'm very tired and rather cold, but I'm okay. Perhaps I shall sleep a little soon. But it doesn't matter about me. You go on. You must hurry.'

He stepped out of the car, closed the door as quietly as he

could and moved alongside the rickety, tree-lined fence that bordered the eastern side of the garden of Crispin's House. On his soft-soled shoes he made hardly any sound. In his hand he carried the torch, switched off; he wouldn't use it unless it was absolutely necessary. For the moment it was not.

Peering to his right in the moonlight he continued on, looking for a break in the fence; he knew there were several throughout its length. Eventually he found what he was seeking. The gap was just wide enough and he squeezed through. The bushes on the other side tore at his hands and clothing but he paid no heed and pushed on until he found himself on the rear lawn. Before him was the house – showing a light behind the curtains of the bedroom's side window. Without hesitating for a moment he ran over the grass to the back door. It wasn't locked. He let himself in and hurried through the darkened rooms to the hall and then up the stairs.

When he reached the bedroom he opened the door to find Rowan standing wide-eyed against the opposite wall. Immediately, as he entered, he saw her expression change from fear to relief.

'Hal . . . I thought it was someone else,' she said as he went towards her.

He wrapped her in his arms and she clung to him. 'I was sure you wouldn't come back,' she said. 'I was certain of it.'

He held her more tightly. 'I shan't ever leave you again,' he said.

'You promise?'

'I promise.'

For a second they remained quite still, then, holding her from him at arm's length, he said urgently: 'Now listen, carefully. We're leaving now. For London. There's no time to waste. There isn't even time to explain why.'

She stared at him and then gave a little laugh which abruptly ceased and he could see his own fear so clearly reflected in her eyes. She knew well that he was in deathly earnest.

'Something's happening, isn't it?' she said. 'I know it.' Her hysterical laugh came again. 'I looked from the window not

long ago and saw Mrs Palfrey and Tom Freeman standing near
the gate, looking up at the house. *Why?* What for? What do
they want? Hal – I'm afraid!' Her rising terror brought his own
fear surging.

'Are they out there now?' he said.

'I don't know. *Tell* me – what's *happening?*'

'Later.' He forced his voice to sound calm. 'We've got to get
out of here.'

'Yes.' She nodded then pulled away from his impelling
hand. 'Just let me put some clothes on. And my case – I packed
it ready to go up to London tomorrow – to find you at the
club.'

'Forget it.' He reached out and took her hand again. 'Just
come as you are.'

With one more look at her bewildered, frightened expression, he turned towards the door. 'We'll leave the lights on in
here,' he said and then led her, hurrying, onto the unlit landing. Side by side they went down the stairs and through the
lower rooms to the kitchen. At the back door he stood listening for a moment, then, carefully easing it open, he pulled her
behind him out into the night.

Hand in hand they raced silently over the grass and she followed him through the shrubs to the gap in the fence. Another
few moments and they were outside on the verge of the road.
In the moonlight he turned to look at her as she stood panting
beside him. Then, tightening his grip on her hand he turned
once again and led the way to the car.

And then they were inside. They had made it. Now they
would be safe.

As the relief swept over him he saw Rowan start as she
caught sight of the huddled figure on the back seat.

'Who is it?' she asked, turning, peering into the gloom. 'It
looks like – is it Miss Carroll?'

'No, it's not Miss Carroll.' He reached down for the keys.
'It's Alison.'

'*Alison?*' she said. '*Alison?*'

He was hardly aware of her cry that followed. He was feeling for the ignition key and finding nothing there. The panic back and sweeping over him he turned to her as his groping fingers searched the floor. She was sitting pressed against the door, eyes wide, staring in horror. He straightened and, eyes following her gaze, looked at the still figure in the back.

He had assumed that she was sleeping. She was not. Even in the deep shadow he could make out her unblinking, unseeing eyes. He stretched out his arm and touched her shoulder. She didn't move. When he brought his hand back he could feel on his fingers the warm stickiness of blood.

For a moment he was paralysed with terror, then, leaning quickly across he jerked Rowan aside and flung open her door. 'Get out!' he yelled at her. 'And *run*.'

They had only gone a few paces when the people came.

Dark, darting shadows, they leapt from the cover on either side of the road. There seemed to be so many of them. As Rowan screamed Hal whirled her about to face the way they had come.

But they were there too, the people. It didn't matter which way you turned, there was no way of escape.

30

When Rowan opened her eyes she lay there for some seconds before becoming aware that she was lying out in the open, looking up at the sky. She tried to get up but found she couldn't. Her hands and feet seemed to be tied.

As her panic threatened to engulf her she closed her eyes again. She hadn't awakened, she told herself. She was still asleep. She must be. Soon she would really awake and find herself at home in her bed, with Hal, safe, and laughing over a bad dream.

But the present sensations wouldn't go. They only grew stronger. And then she began to remember. She'd run from the house with Hal. They'd been caught. On the road a pad of something had been pressed over her face. That was the last she had known, until now. And now here she was. This was no dream. This was real. Silently she lay there and screamed.

When at last the screaming inside her head had died away to a whimper she became aware of the sounds from outside. There was a constant hum of voices all around her – low, but charged with a strange, suppressed excitement. Opening her eyes she saw about her various people from the village. Miss Allardice stood chatting with Sandra Cassen. There was Mrs Palfrey with David Lockyer. She recognized, too, Endleson the vicar, and McBride from The Swan. There were many other faces she knew but couldn't put names to. The schoolmistress was there passing round toffees whilst the butcher tipped a silver flask to his lips. One young man was drinking from a bottle of Coke while the girl next to him bit into an apple. The scene was lit by the wavering, shifting light of lanterns, either held in the hand or suspended from ropes supported by poles. The whole thing was like some strange festive occasion, some weird party.

The surface on which she lay was cold and hard. And then, looking at the lanterns once more she recalled the lights she had seen from the window of Crispin's House. She was on the Stone. She couldn't be anywhere else.

Turning her head to the right she saw Hal lying at her side, just a few feet away. His eyes were closed and he lay very still.

'Hal . . .'

She called his name but he didn't move. She spoke again, louder.

'Hal . . . Hal . . .'

As she strained her neck to stare at his unmoving profile she realized that the voices around her had died away. Shifting her gaze she saw that the faces now were all looking in her direction, eyes full of curiosity. The people continued to regard her in silence for some moments, but then their attention wavered and the chatter broke out again.

Glancing over to her left she recognized the slim figure and blonde hair of Alison, and into her mind flashed a picture of the dead woman she had seen on the back seat of the car. It was Miss Carroll who had lain slumped there; she knew that. Yet Hal had said no, it was not Miss Carroll: it was Alison. But that couldn't be. That was impossible. How could it be? She had seen Miss Carroll there with her own eyes – just as clearly as she now saw Alison standing on the arm of Ralph Collins.

She turned once more towards Hal. His eyes were still closed. From her left she heard a familiar voice.

'Don't worry about him, Rowan. He's all right. He'll come round soon.'

She looked up towards the voice and saw Paul Cassen standing above her. As their eyes met she felt her lower lip tremble. Fighting back the tears that threatened she said pleadingly:

'Paul . . . help us . . .'

He shrugged. 'I'm sorry. There's nothing I can do.'

'*Please* . . .'

He said nothing. After a moment she asked:

'What's happening? What are they going to do with us?'

'. . . It'll soon be over.'

'But what's going to happen? Are you – are you going to hurt us?'

The answer came from another voice. Suddenly Mrs Palfrey was standing at Cassen's elbow.

'No,' she said decisively, 'not in the least. No one's going to harm a hair of your head. Not one single hair.'

'But – then what do you want?'

'Just don't worry.' The old woman spoke like a nurse reassuring a patient. Then, her tone abruptly changing, she said, 'Look! She's got nothing under her head and nothing over her. This is ridiculous. Who's supposed to be looking after these things?'

'Freeman,' Cassen said.

'Huh, I might have known.' Mrs Palfrey looked into Rowan's face again. 'I'll get you a cushion and a blanket. You'd be more comfortable then, wouldn't you?'

Rowan nodded. 'Please – and for Hal too . . .'

'All right.' Mrs Palfrey sighed and moved out of the line of

Rowan's vision. She reappeared a few moments later carrying cushions and blankets in her arms. Cassen took the cushions from her and placed one beneath Rowan's head. The other he put beneath Hal's.

'There,' Mrs Palfrey said, ' – that's better, isn't it?' She laid one of the blankets over Rowan and tucked in the sides. 'You'll be warmer now.' As she laid the other blanket over Hal she said to Cassen, 'I can't have her catching cold. That would be a fine start.' She tucked in the edges of Hal's blanket. 'By rights,' she said, 'I should leave this to Freeman. If he can't take care of it himself he doesn't deserve anything.' She straightened and looked around her. 'I don't even know whether he's here. Have you seen anything of him?'

'No, not yet.' Cassen shook his head. 'But he'll be here soon, there's no doubt about that.'

'Oh, no doubt at all.' With a toss of her head Mrs Palfrey turned and moved away.

Beyond the voices of those immediately around her Rowan became aware of other voices coming up from below. There must be many more of the villagers down around the base of the rock, she thought; certainly the rock itself couldn't hold a fraction of their number.

Raising her head a little she saw that she and Hal were lying in the centre of the stone plateau. Their heads were towards the overhanging lip, their feet towards the wall that rose up, towering above the lanterns. There, close to the wall, a brazier had been placed, its coals glowing, giving off a warmer light than that from the lanterns above. She also saw a small table there holding assorted receptacles and various other objects.

Laying her head on the cushion again she looked over at Hal. His eyes were open now, wide open and fearful. As she gazed at him across the two-yard gap he turned his face towards her. For a while they just looked at one another, then she saw his lips move in a single, unheard word: 'Ro . . .' Involuntarily her right hand moved within the narrow constriction of the cords that held it – as if she would reach out to him – but she could not and she lay still beneath the blanket.

Paul Cassen had moved around and now came to a halt near Hal's feet. He looked from Hal's face to Rowan's. 'There, I told you he'd be all right,' he said. 'Didn't I say that?'

'Let us go,' Rowan said. 'Please, Paul . . .'

'Yes.' Hal spoke aloud now. 'Let us go.'

'It's not up to me,' Cassen said.

'But they'll listen to you,' Hal said. 'After all, you were the one who found us – who got us to the village in the first place.'

'I was only doing my job.'

'Please,' Hal said again. 'Talk to them. They *will* listen to you; you know they will.'

'Oh, no, they won't!' Another voice broke in here and Tom Freeman came into Rowan's view. Stepping forward he stopped by Cassen's shoulder and stood gasping for breath, one hand pressed to his chest. His speech fragmented by his laboured breathing, he said to Hal, 'What happens to you is up to *me*. And you're going to stay where you are. You've put us to enough trouble tonight already.'

'I'll say,' Cassen agreed. 'You had him worried sick.' Turning to the old man he said, 'We were wondering where you were. Thought perhaps you'd decided not to come.'

'Oh, you will have your little joke,' Freeman said, smiling uncertainly. He patted his chest. 'God, that climb up here. A couple of times back there I didn't think I was going to make it.' He took a deep breath. 'Still, I did. I'm here now and everything'll be all right.'

'You've got everything ready? Your will and everything?'

'Oh, yes.'

'Signed and witnessed?'

'Weeks ago.'

Cassen nodded. 'Weeks ago. Yes, I believe you. Could hardly wait, could you?'

'Well – I'm sure you're no different.'

'No, I suppose not.'

'Well, there you are then.' The old man grinned and then turned his attention back to Hal. 'Did you hear all that?' he said. 'My last will and testament. It's all made out. All legal and

above board. Yes, if anything should happen to old Tom Freeman then – ' He broke off, paused with his head on one side
and then added: '*Guess*. Guess who's going to be the lucky one
when I go . . .'

Hal said nothing. The old man looked over at Rowan.
'Guess,' he said.

When she also remained silent he said, 'Mr Hal Graham,
that's who. He'll come into everything I own. Everything.
Lock, stock and barrel.' He raised his head. 'Isn't that right, Sylvia? And you'll be leaving all your worldly goods to Mrs Graham. Isn't that right?' Turning her head slightly Rowan saw
Mrs Palfrey standing there with a look of scorn on her face.

'Why don't you give it a rest,' Mrs Palfrey said, 'and stop
prattling. Old fool.' To Cassen she added disdainfully, 'He
wouldn't have got anywhere if it hadn't been for me.'

Freeman stared at her for a moment then, assuming a non-
chalant air, said: 'Well, what time is this thing supposed to
start? It's getting late.'

'Dear God,' Mrs Palfrey said, 'you've waited long enough.
Can't you be patient a little while longer?'

'It's all right for you,' Freeman retorted, 'but I don't feel
well.' Turning then from the old woman's scornful expression
he said to Cassen: 'I must go and sit down for a minute.' With
slow steps he shuffled out of sight. Cassen and Mrs Palfrey
watched him go, then they too moved away to join the surrounding throng.

Rowan looked over at Hal. He was gazing at her. After a
moment he said, 'Don't worry. We shall be all right.'

She nodded. 'Yes. She – Mrs Palfrey – told me that we shan't
be harmed. Not in the least, she said.'

As she finished speaking she became aware of a great com-
motion in the crowd and then the descending of a sudden
hush. She looked up and saw that all eyes were now turned
towards the figure of the vicar, Endleson. He had moved
to stand beneath the swaying lanterns, his back to the wall.
Someone over to the left murmured, 'It's starting,' and Rowan
closed her eyes in dread.

31

There had been singing and chanting, the voices coming from all sides and from down below. The sounds had rung out over the hillside. Now, the voices were still again.

Mrs Palfrey and Tom Freeman stood flanking the tall, suntanned figure of Endleson. Lifting his head slightly, Hal found himself looking straight into Freeman's eyes. Likewise, he realized, Mrs Palfrey was standing in a direct line with Rowan.

Turning to Rowan he saw that she lay with her eyes tight shut. Don't worry, he had said to her; it would all be all right. And of course he had lied. Just as Mrs Palfrey had lied when she'd said they wouldn't be harmed. But there, the truth of *her* statement all depended on what was meant by harm.

He closed his eyes and let his head sink back onto the cushion. He was bathed in sweat. He knew what the outcome of all this would be – and the thought filled him with terror. Perhaps, he said to himself, it would be better if he did not know; if Alison had never told him. But he *did* know, and it was pointless to conjecture.

He had most of the answers now – and those he lacked were unimportant. He knew now why Mrs Prescot, their housekeeper, had been replaced – and he could guess at how it had happened. He knew now why ugly or old or infirm strangers were not welcome in Moorstone. Only the young and the healthy were wanted here. People like Paul Cassen and David Lockyer, people like Alison and Mary Hughes, people like Rowan and himself. He and Rowan, they were just two of the endless number that had passed this way. Who knew how many there had been? Who knew how many there would be in the future? There would be no end to them. The whole thing would just go on and on. . . .

And what of those others who had lain here before, he

wondered. Had any of *them* known what it was all about? Had any of them guessed at all? No, they couldn't have. Who could? Ever? It wasn't possible. They must have lain here then just as Rowan lay here now – totally ignorant of what was happening, the reason for it all. The young Cassen, the actor David Lockyer, Mary Hughes the painter – not one of them could have guessed. Alison, for all her suspicions, had not. And now Alison – the Alison he had known – was gone. Just as those others had gone – the real Cassen, the real Lockyer, the real Mary Hughes. And now, tonight, it was to be the turn of Rowan and himself.

He opened his eyes again. He was glad of the cushion beneath his head; it allowed him to see without too much difficulty. He watched as Mrs Palfrey faced the vicar, a teacup and a small bowl in her hands. Freeman, holding similar objects, said peevishly, 'I thought I was to be first. I went to the house first. I got my claim in first.' 'Be patient,' Endleson told him. 'Your turn will come,' while Mrs Palfrey tossed her head and said scornfully, 'Listen to the old fool. Just listen to him.'

The vicar took the bowl from her hand, looked at its contents and said, 'Were these willingly given?'

'Yes,' she answered, 'willingly.'

He nodded, upended the bowl and cast the nail parings into the brazier. Then, taking from her the teacup he asked, 'And this too was willingly given?'

Paul Cassen took a step forward and gave the answer to this. 'It was,' he said, and Hal thought back to the morning when he had sat in Cassen's surgery and watched him take blood from Rowan's arm.

Following Cassen's reply Endleson gestured to Mrs Palfrey and she raised the cup to her lips. Briefly she drank from it then placed it in Endleson's hand. Hal watched as the cup was tipped and red liquid streamed onto the glowing coals. Hissing steam rose in a cloud, its sound joining with a long, deep sigh that came from the throats of the onlookers.

Complete silence. Mrs Palfrey put up a hand and wiped her mouth. She stood quite still for a few moments and then,

giving a little smile at the watching assembly, stepped pur-
posefully forward.

As she did so two men moved out from the throng. One
was Lockyer, the other a tall, dark-haired man whom Hal had
seen on several occasions around the village. They followed
the old woman to where Rowan lay, her eyes still closed. Lockyer knelt at Rowan's head, the other near her feet. Slowly, and
with some obvious difficulty, Mrs Palfrey got down onto the
stone at Lockyer's side.

Hal, watching horrified and helpless, saw Rowan's eyes
open as she heard the sounds of movement immediately
about her. As she screamed in terror he cried out, '*Don't touch
her! Don't! Please don't!*' No one took any notice. While Lockyer held her head the other man gripped her feet. Tied by the
cords and held by the hands she could only writhe and squirm
and scream while Hal looked on, tears pouring from his eyes,
unable to move an inch.

And then, suddenly, Rowan's voice was cut off in mid cry.
Mrs Palfrey, after throwing back her head to take in a great
gulp of air, had thrown herself forward and covered Rowan's
open mouth with her own.

Again and again she did it, the old woman. Lying full length
on the stone, one misshapen hand pinching Rowan's nose,
the other holding her chin, she kept sucking in the air and
then forcing her breath into Rowan's lungs. It went on and
on and on. And all the time it was happening the surrounding
onlookers edged eagerly closer, cheering and stamping their
approval. Party squeakers squeaked, whistles and horns were
blown and bells were rung. It was as if they were watching a
game.

Then all at once, just when the excitement of the crowd
had risen to the point of hysteria, the ritual ended. Mrs Palfrey
took one last, long, deep breath and clamped her mouth once
more over Rowan's. And this time the old woman's body was
shaken by a sudden, violent shudder. Again it happened, and
again. While Rowan's wide eyes rolled in their sockets the old

woman's legs twitched, quivered and squirmed as if she were in the throes of some obscene orgasm. Held by the two men Rowan's body jerked and her back arched. Mrs Palfrey gave a final violent shudder, lifted her face from Rowan's and sank down onto the stone at her side.

It was finished.

The deafening burst of applause that came from the crowd died away as Paul Cassen stepped forward, bent over the women and felt the pulse of each of them. Turning back to Endleson he gave a nod of satisfaction. 'I think it's taken,' he said. The crowd cheered. Then he added, 'But she mustn't be moved . . .' Who was he talking about? Hal wondered. Rowan or Mrs Palfrey? Looking at Rowan he saw that her face was peaceful again, her body as still as that of the old woman beside her.

The voices of the onlookers had fallen now into a general chatter which was marked here and there by little laughs and excited exclamations. Then those sounds too died away and only the voice of Tom Freeman could be heard. 'Now me,' he was saying plaintively. 'Now me. Come on – let's get on with it.' Hal raised his head and looked at the old man as he moved agitatedly about at the vicar's side.

And *now*, he said to himself, it's *my* turn . . .

The same procedure was to be followed, Hal saw.

Freeman, barely able to contain his excitement, stood pale-faced, cup and bowl in hand, before the vicar. Endleson reached out, took the bowl, looked into it and solemnly asked: 'Was this given willingly?'

Freeman looked anxiously over into the ring of onlookers and gave a grin of relief as Cleary the barber raised his hand. 'Oh, yes, it was,' Cleary said. 'Yes, indeed.' Then, while Freeman beamed his approval Endleson nodded and turned with the bowl towards the glowing brazier.

Beyond the words of the ritual Hal had gradually become aware of a growing murmur coming up from the hillside and down around the base of the Stone. Now, as he listened, the murmur erupted and the air rang with the clamour of excited voices. Endleson, holding high the bowl, stopped, frowned and looked over towards the steps. The next second a man, a stranger, had pushed his way through the crowd, strode forward and snatched the bowl from the vicar's hand. Turning then towards Freeman, he calmly relieved the old man of the cup.

After a moment of stunned silence the people once again all seemed to be talking at once, though above their voices Tom Freeman's could be heard as he cried out over and over, 'What's happening? What's going on?' And then, near the top of the steps, the crowd parted and three men appeared, side by side. The one in the centre was being carried by the other two, sitting on the seat of their linked, crossed hands. Moving closer to Endleson the bearers stooped and placed their burden on the stone floor, then stepped back. The man sat there, supporting his twisted body on his arms, his single leg thrust out before him. Hal stared. There was something about the face. Like the body it was grotesquely disfigured, but still it retained the trace of something that was familiar to him. Then, in the same second that realization came he heard a voice on his right murmur the name of Lewis Childs.

Lewis Childs. So he had managed to return after all.

As he looked at Childs Hal became aware that Childs was looking at him. Even from this distance he could detect the gloating, covetous expression. He turned away and shifted his gaze towards the figures of the women who lay on his left. Rowan and Mrs Palfrey. Still neither one had stirred. Lying side by side, they looked to be asleep.

'It's not fair!'

Tom Freeman's voice rang out and Hal turned to see him struggling in the arms of Childs's bearers. He saw Endleson gesticulating, nodding and shaking his head, obviously trying to reason with the old man. It was doing no good, though. Freeman, ashen now, was fighting with all his strength to be free. 'It's not fair!' he cried again. '*I* staked my claim. I was there at the house the whole time. It's not fair.'

And then Lewis Childs turned and looked up at the vicar. 'Get on with it,' he said.

The bowl and the cup were held out. Endleson paused, gave a nod, took the bowl in his hand and threw the shorn hair onto the coals.

His words almost drowned by Freeman's desperate, whining cries, Endleson took the cup, held it up and asked: 'And was this also willingly given?'

Paul Cassen stepped forward. 'It was.'

Endleson stooped and handed the cup to the man on the floor. Childs drank from it and handed it back. Next moment the rest of its contents had been poured into the brazier.

Heart thudding, Hal waited.

His time was here; now.

As Cassen and Cleary came to him to take a grip on his head and legs he saw Lewis Childs begin his slow, clumsy progress across the stone floor. It seemed to take forever. Grunting and gasping the crippled man moved towards him, slithering along like some great injured reptile.

But then at last he was there.

Hal looked up as Childs's face loomed above him. He looked into his eyes. One of them was quite blind.

Childs's head went back and he sucked at the air. When, the next second, he brought it down again his mouth was still wide open. Hal felt the open mouth close over his own and cling there, like a leech.

32

He dreamed that he was floating, flying. He had soared upwards at first, high above the hills, above the clouds. There he had hovered for a long, long time and then slowly drifted down again. Breaking through a layer of mist he saw himself lying below. I must get back, he thought.

Then, opening his eyes he realized that he was still lying on the high plateau of the Stone. He saw the people there, all standing around, staring. Suddenly the memory of the nightmare came to him.

Aware of movement closer to his left he turned his head. Right beside him lay a discarded blanket and cushion. Beyond the cushion he saw the girl's face. Rowan's face. He found that the judging of distance, visually, had suddenly become difficult, and then he realized that he was seeing with only one eye. He could see her, though. That face he loved so well. The blue eyes. The heavy, dark hair – untidy now and falling tousled about the smooth cheek. He saw Lockyer there too, bending low, taking off the girl's blanket and untying her bonds. He watched as she smiled up into his face, as he gave her his hand and helped her to her feet. She stood there in her slippers, nightdress and blue dressing gown, chafing the circulation back into her limbs.

'Rowan –' he said, and realized that the voice was not his own.

She reacted to it, though – turning, glancing at him and then back to Lockyer. Laughing, she said, 'Rowan – yes – I must get used to that name now.' She looked down at Hal again. Her brief glance was at once cold and pitying. Then, on Lockyer's arm she began to move away.

Turning, he saw close by him the old figure of Mrs Palfrey. She was sitting on the stone floor, staring after the form of the young woman. In her horrified, bewildered eyes he could see that realization of the truth was dawning.

Looking towards the wall he saw Lewis Childs standing talking and laughing with a group of villagers. He's wearing my clothes, he thought; my face, my body . . . Lowering his eyes he looked down at the body that was his own *now* – at the ugly, crippled form that had so recently belonged to the other. Now it was Childs's no longer; now it was his. He had known it would happen, but the knowing hadn't prepared him for the horror of the reality.

'Help us . . .' he called out.

It had all been for this – as Alison had told him it would be. Now Childs could continue his chosen life; – just as Mrs Pal-

frey could have her life again – this time in Rowan's body and
with Rowan's name.

'Help us,' he called again. And still no one came. No one
even looked his way. Many of the people were leaving the
plateau, he saw. The ceremony was over. In twos and threes
they were moving towards the steps. Soon they would be back
in the comfort of their homes. Among those remaining was
Tom Freeman. Over by the brazier with its dying coals Hal
could see the pathetic, defeated old man. Freeman kept crying
out that he had been cheated. But no one listened.

'Hal . . . ?'

He turned at the sound of his name and saw once again
the old woman who sat on the stone nearby. As he looked into
the stunned eyes he thought briefly of Miss Larkin as she had
stood on the edge of the chalkpit. The look in the eyes was the
same. Now he knew that when he had faced the old woman
that day he had in fact been looking at the horror and bewilderment of the young Mary Hughes. It had been *her* spirit
there; her soul, her mind, her personality – her talent, too; all
of it trapped in an old, cancerous, discarded shell of a body. No
wonder she had made such a choice.

Now, looking into *these* old eyes – the eyes of Mrs Palfrey –
he could see Rowan there, see her misery so clearly. She didn't
understand it – she never would – but she knew the truth, finally.

'Hal . . .' She spoke his name again as he looked at her. He
nodded.

'Yes, it *is* me,' he said.

She continued to stare at him for a moment or two, then,
her voice cracking she looked down at her body and said,
'What have they done? What have they done to us?'

There was nothing he could say. After a while he closed his
eyes and let his head sink back onto the stone.

'Lewis . . . Lewis . . .'

The voice spoke the name several times before he realized
that it was being addressed to him. He opened his eyes and saw
Paul Cassen standing above him. Cassen knelt beside him and
Hal turned his face away.

'It was necessary,' he heard Cassen say. 'It had to be.'

Hal didn't answer. After a moment Cassen went on:

'Look – in a few minutes they'll come to take you home. Both of you.'

'Home?' Hal looked at him. '*Home . . . ?*'

'Yes, well – they'll take you to Primrose House. You'll be looked after there.'

'Yes, and labelled insane – like all the others.'

Cassen shrugged. 'Would anyone, outside, believe you?' He paused. 'But you can continue with your writing there – if you want to. And you can have all your old gramophone records too.' He looked over at the old woman and then back to Hal. 'Anyway, at least you'll have each other.' He got up then and brushed the dust from his trousers. Behind him the remaining villagers were taking down the lanterns. 'I must go,' he said. 'But listen – just – just try and relax. Try and get used to it.' He turned and walked away.

Hal looked over to the woman. She was sitting staring into space, little misshapen hands curled in her lap. Rowan. This old lady with the wrinkled skin, snub nose and frizzy hair. Rowan . . .

He tried to sit up and found he couldn't. This body, this ruin of a shell in which *he* was clothed, was now a part of himself.

'Ro . . .'

She turned her dull eyes towards him.

'Help me,' he said.

Slowly, as if waking from a dream, she got up, came to him and bent above him.

'Help me up,' he said.

Silently she knelt beside him. Her muscles straining, she pushed him up into a sitting position. Then, slowly, he turned and began to propel himself along. She crawled at his side. When he fell she helped him up again. No one called for them to stop. No one seemed in the least concerned.

When at last they reached the rim of the plateau he lay for some moments gasping for breath. Then he raised himself up on his forearms and peered over the edge of the lip into the space below. He could see nothing but the darkness. 'Am I in the right place?' he said.

'What?'

'It *is* a good way down, isn't it – at this point?'

'Yes. And there are rocks underneath . . .'

With her help once more he moved so that he was sitting on the very edge of the lip. She sat beside him, supporting him with one arm. Their feet hung down. When he reached out to her she put her free hand in his. Her face was lit by the light of the remaining lanterns; through his tears it was little more than a blur.

'I shall be all right now,' he said.

'Yes.' She nodded. She pressed his fingers so hard that it hurt. He was glad of that little pain. For a moment they sat without speaking, then he said:

'Go back now.'

'Without you? No.'

'Please . . . Go back.'

She shook her head. 'You promised you would never leave me again.'

He nodded. He turned his face to hers and kissed her on the mouth.

'Ro . . .' he whispered.

For a moment they clung to one another. Then, as if reacting to some unseen signal, they pushed off with their hands.

They fell into the dark, heading for the light.

THE END

Printed in Great Britain
by Amazon

40757721R00111